THE VIGILANTE

by

Jonas Saul

IMAGINE

The Sarah Roberts Series

Dark Visions (One)
The Warning (Two)
The Crypt (Three)
The Hostage (Four)
The Victim (Five)
The Enigma (Six)
The Vigilante (Seven)
The Rogue (Eight)
Killing Sarah (Nine)
The Antagonist (Ten)
The Redeemed (Eleven)
The Haunted (Twelve)
The Unlucky (Thirteen)
The Abandoned (Fourteen)
The Cartel (Fifteen)
Losing Sarah (Sixteen)
The Pact (Seventeen)
The Terror (Eighteen)
The Chase (Nineteen)
The Betrayal (Twenty)
Sarah's Return (Twenty-One)
The Hunt (Twenty-Two)
The Delivery (Twenty-Three)
The Trap (Twenty-Four)
The Ultimatum (Twenty-Five)
The Depraved (Twenty-Six)
The Condemned (Twenty-Seven)
Payback (Twenty-Eight)
The Unknown (Twenty-Nine)
Wrath (Thirty)
The Damned (Thirty-One)
The Game (Thirty-Two)

The Decoy (Thirty-Three)
The Disappearance (Thirty-Four)
The Whole Truth (Thirty-Five)
Alex (Thirty-Six)
Parkman (Thirty-Seven)
Darwin (Thirty-Eight)
Aaron (Thirty-Nine)
Remains To Be Seen (Forty)

The Jake Wood Novels

The Immortal Gene (Book One)
The Immortal Target (Book Two)

Standalone Novels

'Til Death Do Us Part
The Drowning
The Woman in the Woods
The Threat
The Spector
The Mafia Trilogy
A Murder in Time
Frequency of the Dead

Co-Authored Novels

Collision Course (Written with Gary Ponzo)
There Will Be Blood (Written with Rania Stone)
The Soulless (Written with Rania Stone)

Short Story Collections

Twisted Fate (Tales of Horror)

Twists of Fate (Tales of Hope)

Dedication

The Vigilante is dedicated to all the readers who love Sarah Roberts. Thank you for your continued support over the years.

One of my long-term friends and golf partner, Alan Penn, has a special dedication in this novel. The Detective in Charge, Alan Lyson, and the FBI agent, Penn Kierian, were both named after him. Thank you, Alan.

I look forward to our next game together.

Be well and get caught reading.

Jonas Saul

Chapter 1

Friday, February 29, 2008

Death is the ultimate reset.

The cycle continued day after day, year after year. Birth, then death, resetting everything but never fixing anything. Healing the errors could only happen with a reset. Nothing could be gained, and nothing allowed to move forward without the reset, which would make things right.

The lessons in the healing were what made it all possible for him. It was why he did it. What he offered his mannequins was something no one had ever offered them before. No one was willing to offer it after either.

Silence. Absolute. A quieting of the soul. Then the reset.

He gathered his tools, placed them in the black medical bag, then folded up the thick plastic sheet they had lain on and stuffed it inside a separate duffel bag. He took one last look around to make sure he had removed any proof that he had ever been there. It wouldn't do to be found out. He wouldn't be able to offer new dolls a reset if a light was shed on his practices. And there were so many more dolls to offer silence to.

Both mannequins in the basement of the abandoned farm, thirty miles from the northern tip of Toronto, lay on the dirty floor as if the cold didn't bother their exposed skin. A winter storm had blown in overnight, covering his tracks from the previous evening. By the time he finished his work and departed for good, the storm that still dropped a wrath of snow from the dark morning sky would obliterate any new tracks within an hour.

"My little pretty ones," he whispered, not wanting to wake either mannequin. "The lessons I teach are for the enlightened. And now you are. No longer will I pay the price. Nor will you because now you're both exalted."

He zipped the medical bag and slung it over his shoulder. After grabbing the duffel bag, he walked away.

At the large wooden doors, he unhooked the chains that bound them and fastened the locks to the handles. Even these tools would come with him. No one could ever see this farm as anything, but an abandoned plot of land with broken buildings and the spirit of the landowner extinguished long ago.

A blast of cold wind and snow assaulted him when he pulled the doors open. His eyes half closed, he pushed into the snow and popped the trunk of his vehicle with the key fob. After dropping his bags in, he slammed it shut and struggled through the knee-deep snow to the car door.

The thought of being stuck out here, his Range Rover

unable to forge a path to the main highway, caused him concern. Instead, he focused on his destiny and how he had fulfilled it every four years on the leap year without mistake or discovery. This was what he was meant to do. If that wasn't true, then why had success been his for the taking?

The mannequins needed the reset in their lives. There was no other way.

There simply wasn't.

Maybe next time, he would help more than just two.

After warming up the vehicle, he returned to the inside of the barn, where he found respite from the bitter wind. A shudder coursed through him. He brushed the fresh snow off his shoulders, stomped his feet near the door's edge, and then scuffed the shoe prints.

After making his way back through the barn, carefully stepping around the snow piled under holes in the broken wooden roof, he descended the stairs into the basement where cattle were once milked and slaughtered. The back door looked out onto a large green field now covered in a white blanket.

His mannequins hadn't moved. They were nestled together, limbs appearing disjointed as if an angry child had tried to break the arms off her oversized Barbie Doll. They lay inside his homemade prison cell, built in the basement of his home, and welded together here before his mannequins arrived. He needed to be certain that upon his exit, neither mannequin would walk or crawl away. The small metal prison assured that.

After removing their clothes, he laid them on their stomachs on the cold earthen floor, bits of straw caught under their light weight, their skin pale in the chill.

"Why are you mannequins so thin?" he asked out loud. "How could the women of today ever match this glorious size?"

But he knew why. They hadn't eaten in a week. When they had arrived, he'd removed their tongues so neither mannequin could talk, which meant they couldn't protest, ask for anything, or scream for help.

It was all about the reset. Putting things right by putting them in their proper place. In the end, he did the right thing. He knew it and could live with that. These two represented six mannequins so far that he'd helped reset in the previous eight years.

To date, none of his mannequins had ever been discovered. At least not as far as he knew.

But now it was time to leave.

"Goodbye," he whispered in the ear of the blond mannequin. He thought he detected movement behind her eyes but dismissed it as imagination.

He moved to the brunette doll, knelt over her shoulder, and whispered in her ear, "It has been a pleasure allowing you to see the error of your ways. Sleep well, my beauties. Goodbye."

This doll's eyes moved.

He got to his feet fast and stepped back.

How?

One eye opened and searched for him. She struggled to find him without the strength needed to manipulate her neck muscles.

He moved into her line of sight. As he did, the one eye watching him widened as far as the lids allowed.

A low moan escaped her chest. Then a shudder passed

through her body, and her eye lowered, the lid remaining open, life leaving the gaze.

"Sleep well, my mannequins."

He moved away, a wide smile playing across his lips. With his fingers wrapped in black leather gloves, he fastened the lock to the homemade prison door, clicked it in place, and tested its veracity. Walking backward, he watched them, feeling a small sense of loss. He would miss his time with them. These two had been fun. It wasn't often he got to take so much pleasure during a reset. The next reset was four years away. Maybe then he would help four mannequins ascend to their rightful place.

He slid an old wooden door into place, shielding his caged dolls from anyone who happened upon the decrepit barn. He rubbed one hand across his bald pate as he turned to leave.

At the exit to the barn, his Range Rover idling behind him, he held the door a moment longer.

"Death is the ultimate reset," he whispered.

Then he closed the door.

Chapter 2

FEBRUARY 20, 2012

Sarah Roberts tightened the scarf around her neck and dipped her face enough to shield herself against the sudden bitter wind.

Torontonians talked about a January thaw that seemed to be a yearly thing, but it was already past mid-February, and there had been no thaw yet—only cold and wind and more snow.

She was on her way to the first task assigned to her in five months. Her sister Vivian had been strangely quiet before Christmas, but now numerous notes had come through —odd, seemingly unconnected messages. Normally Vivian didn't work that way. Somehow, what Sarah was about to do had a bearing on future events, even though Vivian had told Sarah to lie to the people she was about to meet.

The five-month break had served Sarah well. She had been given a chance to visit Parkman in Maine, and when he returned to Santa Rosa, California, she continued on to Toronto, the FBI tailing her the entire time.

She thought it funny how when the Sophia Project men had followed her, they would sit her down, explain their purpose, and even protect her from harm a few times. These FBI men stayed in the shadows, never approaching, never wanting to talk. She had tried a few times, but they had backed away from her and left the area.

But they were always there. At any given time, she could look over her shoulder and see her tail watching, following. When it got annoying, she would lose them. But they would show up again within a day, sometimes even hours.

Who funded this kind of mission? Five months of tailing one girl, with two men on rotating shifts. That was convincing enough that they were seriously interested in her, yet they hadn't initiated contact.

Her step faltered.

Maybe that was why Vivian had been silent all this time.

A quick backward glance couldn't confirm if she was being followed as the snow caught up in the wind, swirled around the roadside trees, and blew across the street, limiting her view to just over ten feet.

The crisis center Vivian told her to go to today came up on her right.

When she got to Toronto, she had shacked up with Aaron Stevens. He hadn't agreed with her decision to come today. They'd argued about it. He appealed that since they were together if something serious needed handling and Vivian gave Sarah the information on how to handle it, why couldn't

Aaron do it, keeping Sarah safe and out of danger?

Nothing pissed her off more. It was her job to answer Vivian's messages and no one else's. It had always been her job. That was why she had spent the last five months training with Aaron almost daily in hand-to-hand combat. She was ready to deal with whatever came up, confident, stronger, and most of all, healed. Her nose wasn't too crooked after it had been broken in a warehouse in Las Vegas last summer, and the holes where she had been jabbed with a fork had healed up nicely. There was barely a scar.

No one else was meant to handle Vivian's notes but Sarah, and she forbade even the notion that she would involve Aaron.

She stopped in front of the crisis center that was once a house. The outside bore no telltale signs of what was inside. Other than the small sign by the door, it appeared to be like any other house on any other street in the older part of downtown Toronto.

She walked up the shoveled stone steps to the front door, unwrapped her scarf, stomped her boots, and brushed the clumped snow off the bottom of her jeans. Then she twisted the knob and entered the foyer of the building.

A woman stood by a large filing cabinet, rifling through papers. She turned as the door opened.

"Cold one today, eh?" the woman asked.

Sarah nodded, her head hung low, already in the role Vivian had instructed her to play.

After the niceties were dispensed with, the woman had Sarah sit and wait in a comfortable blue chair by a table with magazines. She grabbed one and flipped through its pages. Some of them were missing. She grabbed another magazine and noticed missing pages from it too. Then it dawned on her. They probably remove ads or articles that could be offensive to women or potentially add to the trauma women had gone through before coming to a place like this.

The woman returned and escorted Sarah to a room down a thin hall where another woman would join her momentarily.

Sarah entered the room and unzipped her winter jacket. The carpeted room was bright, with a main light suspended from the ceiling and two other lights affixed to the wall. Blue chairs sat in each corner, similar to the ones in the foyer. She took the seat farthest from the door.

It unsettled her to be at a crisis center under false pretenses. Since Vivian had spoken through her hand in a fit of automatic writing two days ago, she had struggled with the notion of lying to people who help the weak in their time of need.

She couldn't determine Vivian's purpose. But in the end, it wasn't her job to determine what Vivian was up to. As long as Sarah did her best to respond to the messages as accurately as she could, everything would work out as it always had— minus the odd broken nose and bullet holes.

One night a few months back, Aaron and Sarah had counted each other's wounds and scars. Sarah had more than double Aaron's, even though he had been shot multiple times almost two years before in Greece.

She reminisced on their relationship because maybe they had gotten too close. She needed to be available for Vivian. It had become her job, her life. With Vivian's recent silence, Sarah had gotten comfortable, easing into a daily life of shopping, cooking, and tending to day-to-day tasks, a life she hadn't had since Vivian's first messages almost eight years ago.

She even had a chance to finish the first draft of her memoirs. The story of her first kidnapping, *Dark Visions*, was now written and ready for an editor. The second book in her memoirs was called *The Warning*, a name she chose because of Vivian's warning to stay out of the religious commune she entered in pursuit of a horrible man named Armond Stuart.

She'd had time to reflect, look inside, and see what was important to her and what wasn't. She had realized exactly who she was and how that translated in the real world.

Nothing about who she had become bothered her, but she knew others wouldn't like it. Most of all, it was Aaron's opinion that mattered. She only hoped Aaron could grow to accept her for who she was and what she did without question because every day, they grew closer, more intimate. For the most part, she liked it. But getting that close presented problems, like their recent argument about Vivian's messages and his alpha-male response to wanting to protect her and handle the messages himself. That was not how it worked.

Besides, he couldn't come to a women's shelter and do what Sarah had to do today.

Hopefully, he would learn to trust that side of her.

The door opened, and an older woman stepped in with a concerned smile, her aura soft and gentle. She eased the door shut and quietly moved to the blue chair by the door.

"My name is Jennifer," the woman said as she took her seat. "But you can call me Jenny." She paused, then lowered her voice and asked, "How are you feeling?"

Sarah shook her head back and forth.

"Not good, huh?"

"No," she whispered, looking down at the carpet between her wet boots.

"Do you want to talk about it?"

Sarah waited until she thought the woman would ask another question, then said, "He hit me."

Jennifer waited.

Sarah turned in her chair and stared at Jennifer.

"Can you see my nose?"

Jennifer nodded. "Yes. It looks like it might have been broken."

"It was broken."

"Have you notified the police?" Jennifer asked. "Did you provide them with a statement? Or is coming here your first step?"

Sarah looked away, acting ashamed.

"I can't go to the police. He said he would kill me." Her eyes watered by force of will. She met Jennifer's gaze, widening her eyes. With her teeth together, she whispered, "And I believe him."

"We can help from the moment you walk through our door until the day the courts reach a verdict and beyond. I assure you, he can't get to you now. With our help and your statement, we can have him dealt with. If you currently reside with him, we can get you into the shelter until more suitable arrangements can be made for a more permanent residence." She paused again. "I can bring in an advisor to guide you through the justice system and the process of pressing charges. We give you a number for purposes of anonymity, and one of us will become your contact. Think of it like a sponsor helping you through the tough times. Would you allow us to have a medical done? It would help to catalog the marks and bruises. Sometimes as the bruises fade, we forget how bad it really was."

Sarah stood and removed her winter jacket, and began unbuttoning her shirt. Without saying a word, she opened her shirt, exposing her white bra and the litany of scars on her abdomen from years of answering Vivian's messages.

"He has shot me, stabbed me, and burned me. He has connections. I've tried to leave before, but he always finds me. Do you really think the police could stop a man like this? Do you think a women's shelter would protect me from him because I don't?"

Jennifer's eyes had widened slightly at Sarah's candid display. She composed herself as she cleared her throat.

"We can help," Jennifer said, her voice less convincing. "No man is above the law—"

"You haven't met my man," Sarah said as she buttoned her shirt back up.

"You sound like you're not interested in help."

"Oh, I'm interested." She sat back down. "But I'm not convinced anything will help."

"What can I say that would convince you? With the proof of his actions on your skin and a sworn statement, the police could arrest the man in question today. He would be off the streets and unable to hurt anyone else. Your shelter would be confidential. No one would ever know where you are. *He* could never find you."

Sarah looked around the room and then stared at nothing.

"It's all my fault," she whispered.

"It is never your fault when someone decides to abuse

you. You can't make him raise his hand."

She turned and glared at Jennifer. "My father beat my mother and me, and no matter how often I told a teacher or an adult, nothing was ever done about it. The asshole alcoholic went on to drink himself to death. I grew up bitter, hating men but desiring them, needing them." The lies went deeper. She was happy her loving father never had to hear this.

"That still doesn't excuse what this man has done to you," Jennifer said, looking more and more uncomfortable.

"Yes. It. Does."

"I'm curious." Jennifer leaned back in her chair and looked down her nose at Sarah. "Why are you protecting the man who did this to you?"

"You're new here, aren't you?"

That caught Jennifer by surprise. She adjusted in her seat and rested her elbows on the armrests.

"I'm not new, but this is about you and why you came here today. We can talk about me another time. I would like to help you. Coming here today, telling me a part of your story displays a desire to get help. I'm only questioning why you're still fighting it. Or are you fighting yourself? You are safe here. You can let it go. It's over."

"Maybe this was a mistake." Sarah stood and zipped up the lower part of her jacket. "I caused this."

"How do you figure?"

"I taunt him. I go too far. When he gets home late from work, I ask who he's been fucking. It drives him crazy. One night, I cooked for him, made everything all special, then threw the lasagna on the floor and told him to eat off the kitchen tile like the dog he is. That one got me knocked out for hours." She moved toward the door. "So, do you see? Maybe this was a mistake. Maybe he wouldn't hit me so much if I could only learn to control my jealousy and my mouth. Maybe if I'm nicer, he will be, too."

"It's not your fault," Jennifer repeated as she swiveled in her chair to watch Sarah. "There are lots of relationships that go through problems, issues that may even need counseling, but violence is never the answer."

Sarah remained at the door. She looked Jennifer up and down, happy there were people like her helping the weak, sad that she had to lie and make up this story because Vivian told her to.

According to Vivian, coming here today and fabricating a story would save other women's lives and stop something called the "ultimate reset" from happening again.

The ultimate reset? What the hell is that?

"He'll kill me," Sarah whispered at the door.

"He can't if you stay here and let us help you."

"It's my fault," she repeated. "I did this." Fake tears moved down her cheeks. "I deserve what he's done to me. And maybe, just maybe, if he ever kills me, it will be because I deserved that too."

"There's a way out of this. You can stop it. Please let us help you."

"Coming here was a mistake. I'm sorry."

"No, it was the first step in healing."

"Don't be contrary for contrary sakes," Sarah snapped.

Jennifer's hands came up. "I'm sorry. Please forgive me, but I was only stating—"

"Go ahead, invalidate my point now." Acting crazy was never too hard for her. "You people don't understand me. You never could. You haven't walked in my shoes. You don't know me." She wiped the tears off her cheeks as anger replaced the crying. "Just for a minute, I wish you could look inside my life. Then you would know how I torture men, too. I'm just as mean, just as horrible. But because he raised a hand, he goes to jail, and I get a free pass to move on to the next man, willing, ready, and able to be tormented. No, no thanks. I'll stay right where I am until he either kills me or leaves me." She opened the door and stepped into the hall. "What a fucking mistake coming here. I actually thought you people could help."

She pivoted on her heels and bumped into a woman being escorted to another room.

Shit, didn't mean for someone who really needs help to hear that.

She wanted to whisper an apology but instead met the woman's blackened eyes and instantly saw her broken spirit.

Chances are, she didn't hear me.

Their shoulders brushed as she passed Sarah in the hall. Then she disappeared into another room.

Jennifer stood behind Sarah. "If you change your mind, we would love to help you into a new life. I could arrange counseling."

"No thanks. Tried that once. The counselor just wanted to discuss my parents and my childhood. Another waste of time." She started down the hall toward the front of the house. "Thanks, Jennifer. I'm sure what you do is helpful, but you can't help me. I shouldn't have come today. I'm sorry for wasting your time."

Jennifer followed her up the hall. "I assure you it wasn't a waste of time, and if you change your mind, I'll be here."

When Sarah reached the door, she zipped her jacket up and wrapped her scarf around her neck. After pulling her hair clear of her jacket, she opened the door and stepped outside. With one last look behind her, she saw Jennifer watching her exit.

A thought dawned on her. If they ever found out who she really was, they would think it was Aaron, a martial arts expert who she had come to complain about. She prayed that Vivian hadn't set things in motion that would hurt Aaron. Even though they didn't know who she was and could never find her, it was still disconcerting.

She stepped off the porch. The snow had left a new film on the shoveled patio stones. When she got to the gate, a police cruiser pulled up.

Dressed for the weather, the cop got out of his cruiser and placed a hat on his head. The hardness in his face revealed his age. He was either near or past retirement. When he met her gaze, he squinted, the crow's feet on either side of his eyes deepening.

As he walked around the cruiser and stepped onto the sidewalk, Sarah moved aside. He nodded and smiled at her as he moved past to the gate.

At least he's not here for me.

A moment of recognition flashed across his face. He did a double-take, then looked away as if he had violated her privacy.

Nothing about him was familiar to her.

She slipped on her gloves and started walking. In minutes, she had made it down the street and turned down another.

She hailed a cab five minutes later and gave Aaron's

home address.

With the first of Vivian's tasks complete, she had to get home to plan the next one. She had to go shopping for something sexy. Getting a job at a massage parlor was something she never thought her sister would ask of her. It was also something she could never tell Aaron about.

He would forbid it.

It was easier just to go and do what Vivian asked and then explain to Aaron why it was so important. Over the years, it was only Parkman who had ever understood her.

Sarah wondered if her relationship with Aaron would last.

Could she be with someone she had to lie to?

Chapter 3

STAFF SERGEANT ALAN LYSON stepped inside the crisis center's front door and shuddered from the temperature change. He quietly closed the door and moved to the window to watch the woman he passed at the gate. She trudged through the snow as she headed down the street.

"Alan?"

He spun around. "Jennifer."

"What are you up to?"

"Stopping by to volunteer as usual. Who was that girl? The one who just left."

"Unless we're processing her, taking her statement, and pressing charges, I can't tell you. But you already know that. Why do you ask?"

He straightened his back and stepped away from the window as he undid his jacket.

"Anyone here that might want to talk to me?" he asked.

"It's bad. Woman in the back claims to have been beaten by her boyfriend and a couple of his gang members."

"Just beaten?"

Jennifer shook her head. "Evidence of rape, but it's not recent, like in the last few days."

"Hospital involved yet? Examinations done?"

"No."

"I could meet you at the hospital."

"She said she wouldn't leave without a police escort. Since you're the kindest soul around, and I hadn't called it in yet, would you oblige?"

"Fair enough, you got me." He smiled. "But don't forget, I retire in March. You'll have to find another kind soul to volunteer, which means you should start looking soon."

Jennifer walked over, wrapped an arm inside Alan's, and started him toward the hallway.

"Maybe you could recommend someone for us."

He looked sideways at her. "Sure, if you tell me what that girl said to you or if she told you her name."

"What girl?"

"The one who left when I was coming in."

Jennifer pulled Alan to a stop.

"Why is she so important?"

"Because I think I know her. It may sound impossible, but I've seen the look in those eyes before. I recognized her eyes. They're piercing, intense. I'm sure that was Sarah Roberts."

"How would you know her? Have you arrested her before?"

"It's not like that. Remember, I'm a staff sergeant, a platoon leader, and now the DIC, Detective in Charge of a major case. I know a lot about my officers, who they arrest, and who they deal with. I see the mug shots and the arrest records."

"You think she's been arrested by one of your officers?" Jennifer asked.

Alan looked up and down the empty hall. In a lowered voice, he said, "I lost some good cops last summer at that massacre in the mall downtown. When it was all said and done, Detective Waller, one of our force's best detectives, retired because of it. The girl at the center of it all walked away. She left for the States somewhere. Last I heard, she was in Las Vegas. At least that's what the papers said when the Las Vegas Police issued a statement claiming the girl in question had helped them solve a mastermind loan shark murder scam of some kind."

"And you think the girl who left here five minutes ago is that girl?"

"If she was, I want to know. Actually, I need to know. I can't have her running around my city without my knowledge. She's too dangerous."

"Then you have the wrong girl." Jennifer gestured to a door.

Alan didn't move. "Why do you say that? How can you be so sure?"

"Because I saw her wounds. Scars from what looked like stabbings and bullet wounds. She has had a tough go of it. Oh, and her nose was recently broken but healing nicely."

Alan leaned against the wall. "What would she come here for?" he asked, almost to himself.

"What are you talking about? Why else would abused women come here?"

He met Jennifer's eyes. "If it's the same girl I'm thinking of, she's not been abused."

"It sure looked like that to me."

"As far as I remember, the girl I'm talking about broke her nose in Vegas. Those wounds were inflicted on her as she fought a killer. If I'm right, her name is Sarah Roberts. She's a known vigilante."

"She's a *what*?" Jennifer asked, mouth agape.

"A vigilante. Like Charles Bronson in the movie *Death Wish*."

"Never saw it."

"No one is abusing her because no one can." He paused for a moment. "What did she tell you? It's important."

"I can't tell you that—"

The door opened beside Jennifer. She turned around and spoke quietly to one of the other volunteers. The door shut softly.

"She came here for the same reasons every other woman comes here," Jennifer whispered. "At least that was my understanding."

"Then she lied. Something else is going on."

Alan walked back to the front foyer.

"Wait. Aren't you going to help this woman here?"

"Yes, just give me a sec."

Alan called HQ to have Sarah Roberts located and her last known address sent to him. He had questions related to a murder from last summer. At least, that was what he would let everyone think.

Then he would go to her and find out what she was up to.

And ask for her help in finding a killer, a case he was just assigned to.

He was retiring in two months. The last thing he wanted was more dead people on his hands because Sarah Roberts was in town.

He yearned for a smooth transition into retirement, but something told him he wouldn't get it.

What the fuck is she doing in my city?

He walked down the hall and entered the room where a woman sat with two black eyes, his mind elsewhere.

Chapter 4

Special Agent Penn Kierian of the FBI sipped his coffee in the warm front seat of the rented Impala and waited for Sarah to leave the crisis center. He'd called it into his partner, Clint, as they were going to switch shifts soon.

Sarah came out of the building and paused at the gate to check out the Toronto cop. He walked past her, both of them pausing.

What was that all about?

Then she started down the sidewalk at a brisk pace.

He made a mental note to check out what she was doing at the crisis center as he followed a safe distance back. Once she was in the cab, he knew where they were going as the taxi headed toward Aaron's apartment.

He parked in his usual spot and left the engine running for heat. The roads had been cleared pretty well, but the wind and snow showed no signs of abating.

His cell phone rang.

"Kierian here."

"Where is she now?" Clint asked.

"Back home. I have no idea why she went to the crisis center. She didn't stay long."

"Let's just hope it's her sister's doing. We've been on this boring detail too long. I have no idea how much longer they will fund this."

"Don't worry about that. They will never give up on this girl. They'll replace us if we don't get something on her soon."

Clint didn't respond.

"You still there?" Kierian asked.

"Yeah. I'm heading over. You want anything?"

"No. Just my hotel and a hot shower."

"Okay, see you soon."

He dropped the phone beside him and turned the vents up to clear the ice that had started to form on the windshield.

"Damn you, Sarah Roberts," he said out loud to the empty car. "Why are you taking so long to perform your magic tricks?"

They had watched her for five months. Followed her from Vegas. Stayed a week in Maine when she visited that cop friend of hers, Parkman. Many nights, Kierian had sat outside Aaron's dojo and watched him train her in self-defense moves.

In all that time, he didn't see a single act of violence, a warning, or anything from Sarah. No crimes are being solved. No superhero or vigilante stuff. All he needed was one, and then he could grab her. But not until they had proof.

He would need the message as well. However, her sister

communicated with her was critical to his investigation. Orders were orders. They were supposed to stay on her until they got what they came for. Or until they heard differently.

So how did a crisis center play into her life? Aaron wasn't mean to her. Kierian was witness to night after night of dinner and wine, the evening strolls, and the theater. Aaron's home phone was being monitored. They'd received the paperwork within days of arriving in Toronto to set up the tap.

But still nothing.

If she was ever a real psychic or a real automatic writer, Kierian and Clint had seen no evidence of it in over five months.

"All I need is one slip up, and you're mine," he whispered as he stared at the amber light in the living room window of Aaron Stevens's second-floor apartment.

Kierian lifted almost a foot off his seat and banged his knee on the steering wheel when someone knocked hard on the frosted window beside his head.

He shouted and cursed as he opened the door to Clint's smiling face.

"Reporting for duty. Shift-change time."

"You asshole. You scared the shit out of me."

"Oh, sorry about that. Just wanted to see if you were awake."

Kierian got out of the car, pulled his jacket tight around his shoulders, and started away from the Impala.

"When I come back in the morning, I'll see just how awake you are, too," he said. Then he added under his breath, "Asshole."

When he looked back at Aaron's apartment before

turning the corner, the light in the living room was out.

He turned the corner and hustled along the snow and ice-covered sidewalk toward the hotel three blocks away, hoping Clint had seen the light go out.

If Sarah left the apartment and performed a task under Vivian's direction and they missed it, there would be hell to pay.

At least, that's what their superiors had told them.

They could not have a vigilante running around causing havoc. Not anymore. Too many people had died, and not a single charge had ever been brought against Sarah Roberts.

The FBI aimed to change that.

Chapter 5

Sarah let the curtains of the living room window fall back into place. When the men switched places in the driver's seat of the Impala across the street, she was sure it was the same two guys who had followed her since Vegas. She had lost interest months ago, but now that Vivian had her busy again, she didn't want those two sticking their noses where they shouldn't.

They had kept to the shadows for the most part, so she hadn't been able to get too close to their vehicle. But today, in the back of the taxi during the soft snowfall, which seemed to be letting up, with a limited number of vehicles on the road, she had spotted the tail easily.

She remembered the note Vivian gave her to lose them on the highway as she left Vegas. How Detective Collins of the Las Vegas Police Department said that the FBI wanted to talk to her about a "deal."

They tried to follow her out of Vegas, but she soon lost them as her BMW motorcycle had more guts than their fed-issued cruiser.

In Maine, she had noticed them again.

If they weren't going to approach her, she might need to make their acquaintance. Since Vivian had been quiet over the past few months, it hadn't really bothered her that they were there. It seemed harmless. But now that she had errands to run and tasks to perform, she couldn't have the FBI watching everything she did.

It was almost five in the afternoon, and the sun had dropped on this cold, overcast, snowy day. Perfect timing to have a chat with her local FBI agent.

She grabbed her jacket, put it on, slipped into her boots, touched the door handle, and then stopped. A better idea struck her.

Down the hall, in the bottom of the linen closet, she located Aaron's toolbox. She lifted off the top that held nails and screws, picked up the hammer, and shoved the toolbox back into the closet.

Hammer in hand, she left the apartment, locked the door, and started for the stairs. The elevator dinged behind her. The doors slid open. As she swung the stairwell door wide, someone called her name.

Aaron?

The door to the stairwell was almost shut. She turned and opened it again to see him running down the corridor.

"Where are you—" He looked down at the hammer in her hand. "Where are you going with that?"

"To have a chat with someone."

"And you need a hammer to talk? Even after the last five

months of training on street fighting?"

"Old habits. I need the hammer to break the car window. I've done this kind of thing before."

He looked her up and down. "Sometimes you scare me."

"You're not alone. Sometimes I scare myself."

"Can we go back to the apartment and talk about this before you end up in jail on assault charges? Or worse?"

She thought about it, weighing what consequences would cost more. On one hand, it was a perfect time to talk to the agent in the car and find out what their agenda was. The lone male in the car had just arrived and would be alone for some time. On the other hand, Aaron would be angry, and they would fight again. Yet another argument over something that had to do with Vivian.

"You're thinking about it," Aaron said. "Why is there a dilemma? You can't talk first and then solve whatever issue you have using that hammer later?"

"It's not that simple. It's not an *issue I have*."

"Okay, I'll be in the apartment."

After a few minutes of breathing in and out slowly and calming her heart rate, she let the stairwell door close and followed Aaron to the apartment. When she entered, he was sitting in the living room, two glasses of red wine on the coffee table and soft jazz playing on the stereo from their Smooth Jazz Café series.

"What?" Sarah said. "You just *knew* I would come back?"

"I had hoped."

"Watch the assumptions with me. You don't want to be surprised."

She set the hammer down on the little table by the door

where they always placed their keys.

Something about living together had been fun and new. But there was also something about it that was starting to rub her the wrong way.

"Come sit." Aaron patted the cushion on the sofa beside him. "Let's talk about this."

"Why are you home already?" Sarah asked.

"To save your ass."

"Starting the conversation like that will only get you kicked in the teeth. Then we'll see how well you talk." She walked over and looked down at him, her insides roiling. "Do not fuck around with me today."

He looked up at her, his face soft and caring. Then he patted the cushion again.

She moved around the coffee table and sat down.

"Are you going to answer my question?" Sarah asked.

"I'm home a couple of hours early because Daniel is taking over my classes. He wanted to give me a break so I could spend time with you. You seem different the last few days. You haven't been yourself." Aaron lowered his head, fiddled with his jeans for a second, and then turned to her. "I wondered if Vivian had said anything lately, and that was what stirred you up. Have you heard from her?"

Sarah picked up her wine glass and took a long sip. After setting it back down, she lifted one leg under her and faced him.

The only way through this was the truth. He was big enough to handle it, or he wasn't the man for her.

"It started in Vegas," she said.

"You told me everything about Vegas. Didn't you?"

She drank from her glass again. "Not everything."

"What did you leave out?" he asked.

"The FBI."

She started with Vivian's note about the FBI and what Detective Collins had said. She told Aaron that her cousin, Russell Anderson, was supposed to show up in Toronto at some point, but she hadn't heard from him.

Over the next twenty minutes, she explained Vivian's recent messages and how they made no sense to her whatsoever but how that didn't matter. All she knew was that she had to do what Vivian asked of her.

"I guess I'm still trying to wrap my head around the why," Aaron said.

"That's the problem right there."

"What's the problem?"

"You're too focused on the why. If I were too, I would've never gone to Europe pursuing Armond Stuart. He would be free to steal more young girls from their homes and continue his human trafficking business to wealthy men who pay top dollar for sex. I would've never played the role of the victim in the streets of Toronto last summer. Could you imagine your response if the message told you to walk into the middle of a busy four-lane intersection on a green light in downtown Toronto and don't move? Innocent people could've gotten hurt. I could've been killed. Instead, only the bad guys got hurt."

"You're right. I would've never done that."

"Had I not done that, I would be dead right now. The men who pursued me were like ghosts. You remember them. They were there to kill me. Vivian always knows what's best and how to make sure I walk away or crawl in some cases. My job is to follow what she says as closely as possible, and everything will work out."

Aaron cut in. "When I saw you at the stairwell earlier with a hammer in your hand, was that something Vivian asked you to do?"

Sarah sat back and regarded him with a cold stare.

"Are you toying with me? Is this a game?"

"Not at all," he said, raising his arms in supplication.

"I opened up to you about my sister. That's something I hardly ever do with just anybody. I told you everything Vivian has asked of me recently, and you didn't hear a single mention of the hammer. So why ask me that?"

"Why take a hammer to a conversation then? What were you trying to do? What result would you expect?"

Sarah got up from the couch, clutching her wine glass. "I won't talk in circles with you, and I won't be talked down to. By now, you should know that my life is unique. Nothing you can say or do will change who I am or what I do with Vivian. You're either along for the ride or getting off at the next stop."

Aaron stood, too. "Look, I do accept you. But if I could deal with some of your messages, why not give me a chance? Look at how many scars you have. You're lucky to be alive."

She spun around to face Aaron. "These scars are battle wounds. For the innocent lives I've saved. They're for the girls who were freed and who can now go to college and get married, have kids. If that means I have an extra scar, then so be it. For that alone, I ask for another hundred scars." She was almost screaming. "Circumstances are what they are. Evil people, bad people run this planet. Only society keeps the beast inside every man quiet. But once in a while, that beast stirs, and a man or a woman goes astray. I'm honored to be the one who gets to be there when that happens to put things right. Nothing and nobody will ever stop me from being that person."

"Unless Vivian stops communicating, or you die."

"Exactly. But when I die and God, or whoever is up there that you believe in, asks me what I did with my life, I want to say I tried my best. Imagine looking that entity in the eyes and saying I received messages to help someone and decided to go out for pizza instead? Fuck!"

Sweat rolled down her forehead. She hadn't been this worked up in a long time. What was it about this conversation that made her dig her heels in? Was she in love with Aaron? Could she accept that and still be who she was? Did he love her? Was that what this was all about?

"Look," Aaron said in a kinder, softer voice. "All I was saying was that I want to help and limit the amount of danger you face. We don't just live together here. We aren't roommates." He stepped closer and placed a hand on her shoulder. "Or are we?"

"You can't help," Sarah said. She slipped away from his grasp and moved to the living room window. The FBI car was still there, a streetlight reflecting off its windshield. "I agree. We aren't roommates. I have ..." she swallowed the saliva that had built up in her mouth. "I have feelings for you, but it's complicated."

"It doesn't have to be."

"Then leave Vivian out of our relationship, and you and I won't have a problem."

"That's not fair."

"It is, and you know it. Back when I first met you, I got a note telling me to lure my pursuer into a yoga studio. You argued, why not a martial arts studio where professionals could beat him up? At the time, I had no idea why a yoga studio, either. But it worked out, didn't it? Who knows what would have happened if I didn't do what the message said? We argued about that. You walked out. Granted, you followed me the next day, but that didn't help either."

She took a deep breath and looked away from the cold night, turning back to him.

"What I'm saying," she continued, "is you can't get in the way, or try to stop me, or try to do Vivian's bidding for me. She knows you're here, and if she asks something of you, then you can help. So from here on in, I'll be open about the messages, and you just have to step back and accept it. Deal? Otherwise, I'll have to close you out."

"I don't know if I can agree to that."

Aaron walked across the room and disappeared into the kitchen.

"Motherfucker," Sarah whispered under her breath. "He needs a beating on his thick skull. Are all men like this?"

She followed him into the kitchen, where she found him sitting at the table, the light off.

"This thing you're doing tomorrow," Aaron said. "That's hard."

"Sounds like you need time to think about us." She leaned against the doorframe. "Maybe I do, too."

The silence between them held tension. Fighting was a way of life for Sarah, but she didn't want to have to do it with the one man she had really started to feel something for. Aaron had proven himself a true gentleman throughout their relationship. But every time Vivian came up in conversation, or talk of what she had gone through for strangers, Aaron became judgmental and closed up. Maybe he was a traditional man, which appealed to her. But a traditional man could never handle her lifestyle as she performed her automatic writing tasks.

"Maybe this was a mistake," she said. "You get out of a relationship what you put in. When it comes to Vivian, sometimes I have kept her from you. Like these messages recently. If I'm not putting into the relationship, I can't expect much back. But without blaming you, you taught me that."

"How so?"

"People teach you how to treat them. When you got upset about Vivian's note the first time when I met you, you taught me to be cautious about the notes after that. After this argument, I'm not sure we should ever discuss messages again." She paused and switched to the other side of the door frame. "How about this? Every once in a while, I'll disappear for an afternoon, a day, or a week, and then when I'm back, we'll have dinner, watch a movie, and enjoy life. Until the next message, of course."

"I can't do that either," Aaron said. "Not knowing where you are or what you're doing. If you're in danger. Whether I could help or not. What if you were kidnapped again?" His voice raised a notch. "What if you were killed, and they come to tell me while I'm sitting here having a beer scanning Facebook? Or I read it in the newspaper or see it on CNN. How would that feel for me? I'm a professional fighter. I can help you, Sarah."

"We aren't getting anywhere tonight. Let's order something for dinner and forget this for now. Think on it."

"How about we go down and have that conversation with

the men following you?"

"*We* can't. You could get arrested and charged with something."

"And you couldn't?"

"No. They leave me alone. They need me for some reason. Or they're following me to protect me. I have no idea. That was what I wanted to find out earlier."

"Are we getting anywhere with us?" Aaron asked.

Sarah shrugged. "I like to think so. It's you who needs to let my sister go and let me do what she asks. It's who I am. Not accepting that means you don't accept me. Otherwise, I'm good."

A loud knock on the apartment door interrupted them. They looked at each other.

"Expecting anyone?" Sarah whispered.

Aaron shook his head.

She slipped away from the kitchen door and peered out the living room window. The car was still there.

"Toronto Police," a man shouted from the other side of the door. "Open up."

What the hell?

Aaron was already at the door.

"Wait. How do you know it's the cops?" Sarah asked.

He looked through the peephole in the door and turned back to her.

"The uniforms they're wearing."

"How many?"

"Three."

She raised a hand for him to wait, set her wine glass down by his on the coffee table, and crossed the floor to grab the hammer from the little table. Then she retreated to the kitchen.

"Okay," she said loud enough for Aaron to hear.

She watched from the dark kitchen as Aaron opened the door.

"What can I do for you?" Aaron asked.

"Are you Aaron Stevens?"

"Yes."

"Do you know a woman by the name of Sarah Roberts?"

Aaron hesitated, and Sarah could've smacked him on the back of the head for it.

"Why do you want to know?"

Nothing like admitting it.

"We need to speak with her."

"Regarding?"

"That's between us and her. Is she here?"

She could tell Aaron had no idea how to handle that question. The officers didn't wait to hear his answer.

"From where I'm standing, I see two wine glasses on the coffee table, and the lights are low. May we come in? We need to talk to Sarah. If we don't, more women will be tortured and die. Do you want that on your hands?"

Chapter 6

KIERIAN THOUGHT HE HEARD his phone over the live band noise, but by the time he pulled it out of his pocket, the caller had hung up. He checked the call log: Clint.

"Shit."

He left his half-empty beer on the bar and meandered through the tables to the door. Once inside the quieter lobby of the hotel, he redialed Clint.

"What's up?"

"Why didn't you answer when I called? What are you up to?"

"The hotel has a live band tonight. But that doesn't matter. Why'd you call?"

"It does matter. Next week we change shifts. You're doing the night, and I'm doing the day."

"Is that why you interrupted my beer?"

"No. Local cops are here."

"Why? What happened?"

"Nothing that I can see. I haven't taken my eyes off the apartment. A cruiser pulled up out front, and three uniforms got out. All three entered the lobby, buzzed someone, and walked to the elevators. I jumped out of the car to check the floor."

"And?"

"They got off on the second floor. About a minute later, Aaron's living room light went on."

"Have you seen anyone inside yet? Have they come to the window?"

"No. Nothing."

"Okay. It could be nothing. I'll call in and see if we can find out why they're there. I'll call you back."

Kierian hung up and found a chair in the corner by a large fake plant. He sat down and dialed his handler at the Hoover building.

If the local cops were interested in Sarah Roberts, he was supposed to know about it. Nothing angered him more than finding out after the fact.

If they were there for some other reason, then he needed to know that, too.

Nothing would get in the way of what he had to do, and no one would stop him from doing it.

Not even the local police department.

Chapter 7

SARAH SET THE HAMMER down on the kitchen table and moved into the living room as Aaron let the three officers in the apartment.

He flicked the light on and offered them a drink.

As a unit, they ignored him and turned to her.

"Sarah Roberts?"

She instantly recognized the third man. He was the old cop she had seen by the gate at the crisis center earlier in the day.

"What are you doing here?" she asked. "What the hell is this?"

Are they here to arrest Aaron thinking he's been beating me after what I told Jennifer earlier?

"Sarah, when I saw you this afternoon, I wanted to talk to you to find out why you're in Toronto. Then more bodies were discovered this afternoon. Maybe that's why you're here."

She looked at the other two cops. "Do you know what he's talking about?" She looked back at the older cop. "What happened between that woman and me today was confidential. If she revealed any of it to you, then I will claim it was all a lie."

She snuck a worried glance at Aaron, wishing he hadn't come home from work early.

"I'm not here for that. I'm Detective Alan Lyson, and these are two of my constables. I'm here to ask for your help."

"My help?"

"If you're willing."

"I don't work with the police." She moved to the couch and sat down, not offering them a seat. Aaron stayed quiet behind them, still holding onto the partially open door. At least he didn't look scared.

"But you have worked with the police sometimes. The papers said the Las Vegas Police Department holds you in high regard for what you did for them. A man named Parkman, a former officer, would vouch for you, I'm sure. Even my own Detective Waller gave you a glowing report a year ago when you dealt with the Rapturites who killed some of my men in that mall. It looks to me like you do, in fact, work with the authorities."

There was something creepy about someone she didn't know reciting her bio to her.

How the hell does everyone know so much about me?

"We could really use your help," Lyson added. "But we would need to speak to you privately." He glanced at Aaron.

"I guess you didn't hear me right. I don't work with the

police."

The wrinkles on his forehead creased. "But …"

"You may think you know me. Things you read in the papers or on the internet look like I'm helping the police, but I'm not. Half the time, I'm simply trying to stay alive. So, rely on investigative work, and I'm sure you'll catch whoever it is you're hunting."

Her wine from earlier wasn't done. She grabbed it and sipped from her glass.

"The Toronto Police Department has worked with psychics in the past. This wouldn't be the first time."

"What makes you think I'm psychic?"

All three men's boots dried on Aaron's carpet near the front door. Aaron moved away from behind them and leaned against the wall beside the door.

Lyson pulled a notepad from the breast pocket in his jacket. "According to Detective Waller," he stared down at his pad as he talked, "you receive messages and respond to them. In your own way, the perps are either brought to justice or killed." He looked up and stepped toward Sarah. "According to what I've found out online, this is true. And now I need your help."

"Sorry, you've come to the wrong girl. Time to leave."

The officers exchanged glances.

"It takes a lot to come and ask this of you," Lyson said. "I didn't expect our reception to be so cold. Not after what Waller told me an hour ago when I called him."

"I'm curious. What did Waller, the man who once wanted to torture and kill me, say?"

Lyson frowned.

"Didn't know that, huh?"

Lyson said, "He told me to trust you and that you would help. If anyone could help us, it would be you."

"And you believe him?"

Lyson nodded.

"He was wrong. Please leave."

"You don't even want to hear what I have to say?"

Sarah set her glass down and stood. Aaron pushed off from the wall, his arms at his side. She had to manage this because she knew he wanted to show off for her. He would spend the night locked up in a cell if he did.

"What you don't understand is that it doesn't matter what you need from me. I don't work that way. The door behind you is waiting. Use it. I've been kind, but now you're trying my patience."

"Fair enough. But know this. The next murder is on you if you *could've* helped."

"Oh, don't give me that bullshit. By that rationale, every murder I could've stopped is on my head. How do you live with that knowledge yourself? You're sworn to protect and serve. People get hurt and die in this city on your watch. So tell me, how do you sleep at night?" She stepped closer. "What about those girls at the crisis center? Helping them after they're beaten and raped isn't really help, now is it?"

"That's why after I've done a day's work, I stop by that crisis center and volunteer my services to whoever wants to talk. We can't save everybody, but we bloody well try. If I could push a reset button, I would stop every scumbag before they broke the law—"

"What. Did. You. Say?" Sarah's hands tingled as Vivian worked through her, touching her gently and pointing her in the right direction. "About the reset."

"What set you off?" Lyson asked. "I'm here to ask for help, not anger you."

"Okay, time to leave," Sarah said. "Out. Now."

Aaron pushed the door open and stepped out of the way.

A man in a suit and tie stood in the hallway just outside the apartment door, panting heavily.

His shoulders took up the width of the door, almost touching the doorframe sides.

"What the fuck is this?" he asked.

Chapter 8

Kierian ended his call and immediately dialed Clint back.

"Yeah, Clint here."

"Get up there. Remove those cops from the premises. I'm on my way." He ran through the lobby and hit the street, almost losing his balance on the wet and slippery sidewalk.

"Why?" Clint asked. "What happened?"

He could hear Clint running, too.

"I called it in. There is no reason for those officers to be in that building. There is no record of their visit. It wasn't logged or called in. Sarah has history with the Toronto police, and she could be in trouble. I'll be there in five minutes. Get up to Aaron's door and listen in. We have orders to break it up. If the cops give us flack, our boss is clearing it with Toronto's police chief as we speak to have them ordered away from Sarah."

"Okay," Clint said. "I'm in the building now and taking

the stairs. I'll be at her door in under a minute."

"I'm on my way. Don't fuck this up. Keep Sarah safe at all costs, but if there's trouble, use your weapon. Just don't shoot to kill." He crossed a street and jumped over a snowbank on the other side, almost losing his balance again. "They're Canadian cops, and we're the FBI. The paperwork would take us years. Just keep her safe."

But the phone was already dead.

Chapter 9

"NOW, WHO THE FUCK are you?" Aaron asked. "Another cop who wants to use Sarah?"

"May I come in?" the man in the suit asked.

"No, you may not," Aaron said. "Everyone leave. It's time to fuck off."

"There's no need for hostility," Lyson said from behind him.

"Okay, seriously," Aaron said. "Sarah has made her position clear. It is time for everyone to go. We don't need more cops coming in."

"I agree," the man in the suit said.

As Lyson and his constables moved through the door, the man in the suit stepped back to give them room. Sarah walked over to the door, wanting a better look at the new guy to see if he was one of the FBI men who'd been tailing her.

"And who are you?" Lyson asked.

The newcomer pulled a badge and said, "FBI, Special Agent Tower Clint."

A door banged hard down the hall. Everyone turned toward the noise.

"That's my partner," Clint said. "Special Agent Penn Kierian."

Sarah edged past Aaron to watch the exchange between the men.

"Long way from home?" Lyson asked. "You're not even close to your jurisdiction."

Kierian ran up. "How come no one knows of this visit?"

Kierian met Sarah's eyes and then looked away. She was sure of it. These two had tailed her since Vegas.

"Why are you here?" Sarah asked before Lyson, and his men could respond. "Need me for something, too?"

"Not at the moment," Kierian said.

"I just finished telling Toronto's finest that I don't work with the cops," Sarah said. "That means FBI as well."

All six men stood silent, looking at each other until Sarah spoke again.

"How come no one's leaving? Something left unsaid?"

"I want to know what the FBI is doing in Toronto questioning me and my constables. And how would you know whether or not this is an official visit?"

Kierian's cell phone rang. He pulled it from his jacket pocket. When he did, Sarah didn't miss the glint of light reflecting off his weapon in an inner holster by his ribcage.

"Kierian here." He listened for a moment, then extended his hand to Lyson. "It's for you."

Lyson frowned. "Is this a joke?"

Kierian shook his hand in the air, gesturing for Lyson to

take the phone, which he did tentatively.

"Hello?" After a second, he stood straighter. "Yes, sir. I understand, sir. Okay." He handed the phone back to Kierian, who ended the call.

Lyson turned to his constables. "That was the chief. We're to exit this building immediately and not bother the American visitor, Sarah Roberts, or her Canadian friend here." He gestured at Sarah. "Ma'am." Then he started down the hall, his men following close.

"Enjoy your evening," Kierian said and backed away.

Clint followed him.

Aaron moved in close to her. "Aren't you going to ask why they're following you? It looks like they're connected high up."

"Not tonight. At least not while there's alcohol involved."

"Alcohol?" Aaron frowned.

She pulled him inside the apartment and shut the door. After locking it, she sat on the couch.

"Kierian's been drinking," Sarah said.

"Why did you get all worked up about the word reset when that guy Lyson said it?"

"You caught that?" *Well done.* "When I told you about Vivian's message to go to that crisis center, she said it would save other women's lives and help stop the 'ultimate reset.' Put it together. What that cop said about the next murder being on my head, and he chose the word 'reset,' I figure I'm already on the right path. Without anyone knowing it, I'm already helping. Or I should say, Vivian is."

"You don't think you're stretching it a little?"

She ignored the taunt. "Those FBI guys have some

power, eh? One phone call, and the top cop calls his dogs off. What the hell is that?"

"I'd like to know what the hell is going on."

Sarah got up and walked toward the bedroom. "I'm going to bed to read for a couple of hours, then sleep. I didn't shop for new clothes tonight, so I need to get up early."

"Seriously?"

She stopped at the corner of the hall that led to the bedroom.

"What do you mean, seriously?"

"You're still going to apply for a job at a massage parlor where they perform lewd acts?"

"Have you listened to a word I said tonight? Bumping into Lyson at the crisis center got him here tonight. The FBI came running to help. A lot has happened. I have things to think on. Vivian is orchestrating something. So, of course, I'm going to apply for the job tomorrow. Eleven a.m. in North York, just as she said. Nothing changes."

"At least let me take you. I'll wait in the parking lot—"

"Out of the question. And don't follow me, either. We clear?"

Aaron met her eyes and didn't waver. "Fine, have it your way. You're on your own."

Sarah entered the bedroom and disrobed, wondering when would be a good time to leave Aaron. This wasn't working, nor would it.

As long as Vivian gave her messages, she was doomed to be single.

After the light was out, she rested her head on the pillow and stared at her Kindle. Tears wet the pillowcase before she fell asleep.

Chapter 10

SARAH HAD CALLED AHEAD two days ago, so they were expecting her. Massage parlors were almost always hiring and were happy to interview a newbie.

She wore a pushup bra from Victoria's Secret and a low-cut tight top. It was too cold to wear a skirt, and without knowing what to expect at the parlor, so jeans would have to do. Fighting in a skirt could get things exposed too easily.

Her instructions were simply to apply for the job. There was no way in hell she would ever do the job, not even an audition if that was what these people did. Vivian just told her to apply in person at this address at this time. Vivian had done her part. Whatever came up, Sarah would do hers.

The cab dropped her off at the end of the complex. She paid the driver, got out, and looked around for her FBI tail. On the way over, she had tried hard to spot them but couldn't.

Slipping out of the building over the superintendent's apartment balcony was genius.

To be sure she didn't have a tail, Sarah walked away from the parlor, circled the building on the cleared sidewalk, and then crossed the parking lot back to the building. No one sat in a parked car. None of the cars looked like the FBI Impala in front of Aaron's apartment all night, every night.

Her phone said she had three minutes until her interview.

"Here goes nothing," she whispered to herself.

There was something to be said about girls in this profession. She wished for a better life for them. Many of them worked in this profession because they had been abused when they were younger. She had read about the "John School" Toronto had, where men caught buying the services of a sex worker could be sentenced to go there where they would learn more about sex trade workers and realize they were contributing to the pain and abuse of these women.

The front walkway of the massage parlor had been shoveled and swept fresh this morning, ready for the steady flow of customers. The windows were tinted too dark to see in. Just inside the glass, blinds were drawn, ensuring no one saw anything. A neon open sign hung high in the center window, unlit. On the door, a little sign said to buzz for entry.

Sarah hit the buzzer and waited. Being in Toronto since before Christmas, without a word from Vivian, she had stopped carrying her gun until today. Now it dug into the small of her back, a foreign feeling after not carrying it for almost half a year.

The door clicked. She opened it and stepped inside.

Immediately there was another locked door. She pushed on it, but it didn't budge. Trapped between the two doors, she waited.

After half a minute, a woman in her sixties opened the door.

"That's a lot of security," Sarah said.

"You never know who is coming in," the woman said with a European accent. "My name is Rita." The woman stuck out her hand as she examined Sarah's body.

Sarah shook the woman's hand firmly. "Sarah Robertson," she said, the fake name rattling her at how close it was to her own. "Are you doing my interview?"

"Yes," Rita said. "Follow me back to our lunch room."

"When do you open this morning?"

"Now, but I'll wait a few minutes so we can talk. My daytime girls should be along at any minute."

Rita led Sarah past small statues on little pillars, down a dark hall that smelled of incense with numbered doors lining each side. At the end of the hall, a door opened up to a small kitchen.

"Please, have a seat," Rita said. "Would you like tea or a coffee?"

"I'm fine, thanks." Sarah slipped out of her jacket, letting it fall to the couch against the back wall. She sat down beside it, her knees touching. She hated to dress in a way that half exposed her breasts, but Vivian said it was important.

Usually, in a moment like this, wearing a top like this one, nervousness would twist her stomach. But she felt nothing. This was where she was supposed to be and what she was supposed to be doing. She sat back and relaxed in the role.

Rita filled a kettle with water on the counter and plugged it in. She grabbed one cup, dropped a tea bag in it, and turned to Sarah.

"So, tell me, where have you worked before?" Rita asked.

"I haven't. This would be my first time."

"What makes you think you could do this kind of job?" Rita asked.

A little speaker by the door buzzed.

"Please wait here while I see who that is."

"Of course," Sarah said.

When Rita left, Sarah adjusted her top to show less. If the reason she was here didn't reveal itself soon, she would have to leave. The gig would be up. Finding the right answers to an interview of this sort might prove difficult.

Maybe I'm supposed to burn the place down.

Footsteps down the hall announced someone approaching. She straightened her back, reached for her gun in case the person walking toward the kitchen was the reason she was supposed to be there, and stared at the door, waiting.

"As I was saying," Rita said as she stepped into the kitchen. "How do you feel about a job like this?"

The kettle began to whistle. Sarah waited until Rita had unplugged it before speaking.

"I've been out of work for almost a year. Times are tough. With Christmas just passing, it hurt to not have any money. My girlfriend works at The Rose, a massage studio in Etobicoke. She told me how much she makes in a week, which is more than I have ever made at any job in an entire month. For that kind of money, I would do almost anything."

A door opened and closed in the hallway somewhere, making Sarah's head snap toward the door.

"Two of my girls are here. Don't worry. They will

answer the buzzer now."

Sarah nodded.

"Are you aware of what we do here?" Rita asked.

"Massage?"

"Yes, of course, but we offer extra items."

"Extras? Like what?" Sarah asked, trying to sound innocent even though she could assume what *extras* were.

"I'll show you," Rita said. She opened a drawer on the far side of the counter and pulled a piece of paper out. Then she handed it to Sarah.

Her stomach twitched as she read the list of extras. Hand jobs were listed for forty dollars, all the way up to shower massage, duos, and body slides for a hundred dollars.

"Some girls offer full service for more than a hundred, but I will leave that up to you."

"Full service?" Sarah asked, her voice almost cracking at the anger of the position Vivian had put her in.

This had better end fast, or I'm leaving.

"Full service is anything the client wants. You know, sex."

"Ahhh." Something in Rita's face made Sarah want to punch some sense into her. Then she immediately felt sympathy for her.

"Are you able to handle that list? It would be the minimum requirement of employment here. Hardly any man comes through our establishment without wanting at least a happy ending. And we're busy. One girl could see more than a dozen men on an average eight-hour shift."

"What if each man wants full service?" Sarah asked, unable to control herself. "Would the same girl do that as well? To a dozen men in one day?"

Rita pursed her lips, looked away, stirred her tea, and then looked back at Sarah.

"I've had girls who have pulled doubles for me, having sex with random men all day. The more you play, the hotter you act, the bigger the tips they offer. After a month here, you buy a new car. After six months, you put a down payment on a house. But in here, you're safe. This is better than letting the man buy you dinner and a movie, and then you have sex for nothing. At least here he gives you the money instead of wasting it on food."

"This business has hardened you, hasn't it?"

"If you are to work here, you have to know the truth. I won't coddle you. That's what the men are for."

Rita pulled the tea bag out of her cup and dropped it in a garbage receptacle by the fridge.

The buzzer sounded.

"And they start coming early, so to speak," Rita said, smiling as she took the first sip of her tea. "It sounds to me like you have to think about it."

Sarah grabbed her jacket and slipped it back on. "Maybe this isn't right for me."

"I was beginning to think the same thing," Rita added. "I'll see you to the door."

"Tell me, how can you do what you do?"

"Don't come here looking for a job, and then once the job description is given to you, judge me for feeding my kids after my husband walked out for a younger model. I couldn't live off welfare forever. Now, leave. Come on." She walked ahead of Sarah down the hall, her teacup still in her hand. "I would do anything for my kids," Rita said over her shoulder to Sarah. "I would die for them. This isn't half that bad."

She was right. Sarah had no right to judge or look down on her for the choices she had made in this dog-eat-dog world. Whatever the reason Vivian had sent her here, she had done exactly what was asked of her. Now she would catch a taxi back to Aaron's place, get out of these clothes, and take a long hot shower, her image of men greatly reduced.

How could men routinely do this to these young girls?

She wasn't naïve. Prostitution was the oldest profession in the world. After stopping Armond Stuart and his human trafficking ring a few years ago, she knew all too well the horrors that men perform on women and girls. But she alone could never stop it all. Being this close, inside a bawdy house, shook her and made her want to grab every employee and force them outside to go find better lives. It wasn't like the girls Armond Stuart controlled. Those girls didn't have a choice. These women did.

At the front, a scantily clad woman wearing a camisole, panties, and red high heels was admitting a tall, good-looking man with wavy black hair.

What the hell does he need to be here for? He could find a woman easily.

He wore a wedding ring.

Sarah wanted to pull her gun and shoot him in the foot for what he was doing.

Disgusting.

The buzzer sounded. Then again, as if the person was leaning on it.

Rita looked through the blinds and then hopped over to open the door.

"Come in, come in, dear," she said. "Are you okay?"

A woman entered the parlor's front area from the outside.

The other woman with the customer walked past Sarah and down the hall to one of the rooms. Sarah wanted to grab her, smack her face, and wake her up. This was no way to live. The damage these girls were doing to themselves would last a lifetime.

Rita shut and locked the front door behind her and walked to the woman who leaned on her arm.

"He was chasing me …" the woman said through tears as she trembled and caught her breath, her hair in her face. "He said he would kill me for what I did yesterday. I called the police on my way here." She looked at Rita. "I didn't know what else to do. I'm sorry, I had nowhere else to go."

"It's okay, dear. We'll sort this out. He can't get you here."

"He's got a gang." Her voice raised to hysteria. "He won't stop. I don't know what to do." Her knees buckled, but she caught herself, and Rita struggled to keep her upright. "They all want to rape me. If not, then they'll kill me. I can't handle it. I couldn't go through with it."

Sarah quickly stepped in and helped keep the woman on her feet as Rita guided her to a leather chair in the corner.

The woman looked oddly familiar. She raised her face and met Sarah's eyes, widening when they settled on her.

"What are you doing here?" the woman asked.

Rita looked between the two of them. "You know each other?"

"Not exactly," Sarah said. "We bumped into each other yesterday."

"At the crisis center," the woman finished for her. "I finally went in and told them everything Juan and his gang had been doing to me." She sniffled, and Rita offered her a

Kleenex. "They arrested Juan last night."

"Well, that's good then," Rita said. "You're safe now."

Sarah moved to the blinds and peeked outside. If someone was pursuing, this woman and the police were on their way, one or both of them would be here shortly. She wondered if she wanted cops to catch her inside a massage parlor.

"Juan made bail this morning. The volunteer at the crisis center told me to come in, and they would help to relocate me today."

"Are you going there then?" Rita asked. "You can't expect to work today with those black eyes."

"Heartless bitch," Sarah snapped at Rita. "The fuck you say. This girl is not working today. She's running for her life."

"Why are you still here?" Rita turned back to Sarah. "Interview is over. You did not get the job. You can go."

"I didn't come for a job."

"Then why are you here?"

The buzzer sounded loud and hard.

"I'm here to protect her," Sarah said, nodding at the woman sitting on the chair.

The buzzer sounded again. "When this customer's settled in a room, I want you gone."

Rita moved toward the front door. Sarah came around and knelt beside the woman.

"Were they following you? Was it Juan after you this morning?"

The woman sniffled and looked at Sarah. "They were watching my apartment. I was lucky to get away. I think he tracks my cell phone or something. Six blocks from here, I saw him in my rearview mirror. I called the cops—"

What sounded like a firecracker snapped in the air, but Sarah knew it for what it was.

Gunfire.

Before she could grab her own weapon, two more shots were fired.

Rita stumbled backward into the front room, holding her stomach. When she turned around, blood trickled past her fingers. Her eyes were wide, she opened her mouth, and blood seeped past her lips. She wavered on her feet for a second, then dropped to her knees, falling face down on the carpet, her hands never leaving her stomach.

"Come on!" Sarah yelled. "Now!"

Sarah grabbed the woman's arm and forced her from the chair. She was like dead weight, her body almost paralyzed in shock.

Footsteps pounded inside the front behind them as they ran down the hall toward the kitchen, Sarah pulling the woman with her. Sarah kept hoping the woman would stay on her feet for that brief run.

As they reached the kitchen door, a man shouted from behind them.

"I'll kill you, bitch, and everyone else that gets in my way."

Sarah let the woman go inside the kitchen, turned, and slammed the door shut. The woman crumpled to the floor and curled up in a ball, shuddering. Sarah grabbed the knob to lock it, but there was no lock on the door. As fast as she could, even as footfalls pounded down the hall, she grabbed a chair and slipped it under the door handle at the exact second the knob twisted.

She flung herself away from the door and placed her back against the wall, her gun aimed at the ceiling. The woman lifted her head.

"Who are you?" she asked.

"Move away from the door," Sarah whispered. "Do it now."

"Open up, or I'll shoot my way in," the man shouted from the other side of the door.

Being threatened angered Sarah in a way she hadn't felt since her time in Vegas.

"Okay, I'll let you in," Sarah called out. "But you won't hurt us, right?"

"Don't," the woman pleaded, her face a mask of terror.

"It'll be okay," Sarah whispered. "Just get over to the far corner."

"I won't shoot anybody," the man shouted from the hall. "I just want to talk."

"Okay, I'll open the door. As long as you just want to talk."

"That's it. Just talk."

Sarah waited until the woman was far enough away on the floor in the corner. Then she kicked the chair out from under the doorknob, clicked the safety off her weapon, and brought the gun down.

The door clicked open, swinging wide with Sarah staying behind it.

The man stepped into the kitchen, scanned the room, and stopped on the woman curled up sobbing in the corner. Then he turned all the way to the right and caught sight of Sarah, her gun aimed at him.

Before he did anything else, she fired into the lower side

of his thigh.

He wailed and dropped to the floor, his own weapon sliding across the floor as his hands scrambled to his wounded thigh.

"Shoot an innocent woman, eh?" Sarah stepped over him and looked down. "You stupid motherfucker." She brought the gun to about a foot from his face. "I'm going to put five more bullets in your face."

"Noooo!" he shouted, more out of fear than pain.

"One bullet in each eye, one in your mouth to shut you up, and two in the forehead to turn that brain of yours to squash. Then maybe you won't hurt defenseless women anymore."

"No, please don't," the woman in the corner pleaded.

Sarah looked over. "You've got to be fucking kidding me. After what he's done to you. He came here to kill you. He just shot Rita in front of your eyes, and you want me to spare him?"

Blood pumped from his leg wound. If they didn't put a tourniquet on it, he would die whether she did any more damage or not.

In her heart, she knew she wouldn't murder him in cold blood, but the sound of her words consoled her and struck fear in a man who lived by doing that to others. He needed to feel what it was like to be utterly afraid.

"You need to tie that leg off, or you'll die," Sarah said. "But first, are there others outside? Or did you come alone?"

"Alone. I came alone." He gritted his teeth, his face pale, his eyes bugging out.

She touched his cheek with the tip of her gun. "You wouldn't lie to me now, would you?"

"No. Please, no."

She pulled her jacket off. "Tie the sleeves of my jacket tight around your thigh above the wound. Do it now, or you're going to die."

Noises and commotion came from outside the hall.

"Your buddies?" Sarah asked as she brought the gun back to aim at his face.

Before he could reply, a man shouted, "Police!"

"Put down your weapons and come out with your hands up."

"Okay," Sarah shouted down the hall from behind the door. "We're coming out. The man who broke in here and shot the woman at the front isn't a threat anymore. He's been neutralized."

"Just come out with your hands where we can see them."

"Give us a second."

She ran over to the counter and grabbed a paper towel. With it, she picked the man's weapon up off the floor and carried it to the door.

"This is the weapon that shot the woman in the front."

She swung her arm and tossed the gun out into the hall.

"Okay, we're coming out. There are two of us. Don't shoot. We're unarmed."

She flicked her safety back on her own weapon, shoved the gun in the back of her pants, and grabbed the sobbing woman off the floor. She helped her to her feet and guided her through the door, their hands raised as high as they could.

"The perpetrator is in the kitchen with a leg wound. He'll need medics ASAP."

"Come on, come on," the cop gestured.

Behind him, two more cops materialized. More sirens

approached outside.

At the end of the hall, cops grabbed her and pushed both of them to the side, where they were frisked.

"I'm still armed," she said. "I have a permit for it."

The officer stopped on the gun in her pants. His eyes widened.

"I'm not leaving my weapon behind," she smiled. "Too expensive."

"Gun!" the cop shouted. "She's got a gun."

He kicked her legs out from under her before she could react. Two other men jumped on her back, one placing a knee between her shoulder blades. She tried to tell them about her permit to carry and that the gun was expensive, but her windpipe was cut off momentarily. She couldn't breathe and couldn't move from the weight on her. White light filled her eyes.

The gun was ripped from the back of her pants as her arms were wrenched behind her. Cuffs were snapped on roughly, causing enough pain in her wrists to make her think they had broken. Pain ignited her anger. She wanted to tear their faces off, but she still couldn't move. No matter how much Aaron had trained her in close-quarters fighting when the power of three men held her down, there wasn't much she could do.

The knee came off her back. She took a large gulp of air as her shoulders ached from being wrenched back so far. Her eyesight cleared in seconds, but pain flared from several places on her body.

"Get the fuck off me," she shouted. "Stupid motherfuckers."

"Shut up, slut."

They rolled her onto her right hip and, with one man on either side, lifted her up.

"You approached officers of the law with a firearm. Are you a fucking stupid skank? Dressed the way you are, working in a joint like this, I guess it makes sense." He looked at the two men on either side of her. "Take this stupid slut out to the cruiser. When we get to the station, we'll charge her with everything we can." He headed down the hall. She heard him say *stupid whore* before he got too far.

A siren outside came to a stop. Two paramedics rushed in, one going to Rita and checking for a pulse, the other knelt beside the woman with the black eyes.

The cops half walked, half dragged Sarah outside into the brisk February wind without her jacket to the back door of the farthest cruiser.

They shoved her into the back, banging the side of her head on the roof before she got in.

"Serves you right, whore," one cop said as he leered at her cleavage.

She kept her mouth shut. Protesting would only get her more abuse or even pepper sprayed. Assholes like this was one of the reasons she didn't trust cops.

Her wrists ached, her shoulders throbbed, and now she had a wicked headache.

She had done what Vivian had asked of her. If she hadn't been here, there would be two dead women or more.

Getting arrested had to be part of the plan, too.

Didn't it?

Throughout the entire incident, she didn't once consider what Aaron would think. That really scared her.

Chapter 11

ON KEELE STREET, JUST north of the 407 Highway, the man sat in his Range Rover and stared at the hole in the fence—the hole he made in the middle of the night last summer. It was still there. No one had come by in six months to repair it, and no one would.

The fence guarded an empty warehouse. A small metals company used to occupy the warehouse before they relocated to a larger facility in Mississauga. He had done his research. The site was available for lease. Anonymously, he had a real estate agent confirm that there would be no appointments to see the property for the month of February. Come March, he didn't care. The building wouldn't be here anymore.

It was time to let his mannequins be discovered. That was one of the reasons he had chosen a spot so close to downtown Toronto. No more abandoned farms north of the city. No more holes in the ground far from home. Not at his age. He was done with the reset. This was to be his last. He would accept his just desserts as he had made his dolls accept theirs.

Life had consequences and accountability. Today, people were not interested in accepting that. He had seen it all too much in his line of work, and it disgusted him.

That was why he chose the leap year, February 29, every time it came around, to make at least two mannequins accept the ultimate consequence for their actions. After all, it was a leap year. Time to leap ahead, cleansed, and ready for another four years.

Two represented balance. Yin and yang. Removing their tongues stopped all human indignities like pleading, begging, bargaining, and ultimately acceptance. He didn't care if the women accepted what he did to them or hated him for it. Had they lived better lives, they wouldn't have found themselves in their particular predicament.

It was all their fault. They deserved what happened to them. They brought it upon themselves.

He learned a long time ago that every time he was with a woman, there was a price to pay. Whether it was a cash price or a mental price, there was always a price to pay. At the end of every relationship, he had always suffered some kind of loss, so he stopped having relationships twenty years ago. Knowing that going in is fair. But why was there a price? Why couldn't men and women be together without the fee? Men didn't have a price. They just want companionship. What gave women the right?

Women are foreign, enemy, hostile territory.

Virtually, men were at war with them. He saw it all the time at his job. Women didn't get that men were physically stronger, so when pushed, women ended up paying the price.

He made women pay *his* price without ever getting pushed, riled up, or unjustly paying their price. If he didn't let them in, there was never a price to pay. At least not for him.

Yet he was cursed with the natural urge to be with a woman. Month after month, year after year, his urges grew and intensified. Until that fateful day, February 28, the leap year of 1996. He allowed himself to be drawn in on a date even though his sister had advised against it.

But he didn't listen to her.

The woman seemed nice and dressed well. They went for dinner and then had drinks after. He found they had a few things in common. At least enough to ask for another date.

She had drunk too much wine. Things got tense, and the conversation stilted. The clock ticked past midnight. Leap day was upon them. His date explained that it was the anniversary of her sister's murder.

He'd thought if the woman's sister was anything like her, maybe there was a valid reason for someone taking her life.

The woman wailed at the injustice, screamed at him as if he were the murderer, and made a scene in the near-empty bar they found themselves in that night. He'd backed away from her, suggesting that he would pay the bill and they could leave.

She took his backing away as a sign that he wasn't on her side. In her drunken state, she irrationally accused him of being involved in the murder of her sister, which was preposterous.

Then she physically attacked him.

He repelled her as best as he could, but she had liquid

courage and the strength of five women.

The police were called, and he was arrested. She had carpet burns from when he pushed her away. She had smashed her cheek on the corner of one of the tables. The woman claimed he had drugged her drinks to rape and murder her on the anniversary of her sister's unsolved murder.

The leap year is also called the Bissextile Year, and she claimed that was what he had wanted to do—have sex with her as he had with her dead sister.

Within twenty-four hours, he was released, and the arrest stricken from the records once the police had taken everyone's statement, the bartender included.

That one date almost cost him his job, which he was retiring from this year. His life would've been ruined by this one date, by this woman whose price was far too steep to pay.

He had gotten off lucky. He would never allow himself to get that close again.

The woman ended up going back to the crisis center and was lost in the system. He never heard from her again.

He never dated again.

But he was scarred for life.

And every bissextile year, he chose two women to become his dolls for the week leading up to February 29. This one would mark his last leap day. His urges had decreased. He couldn't fix the world two mannequins at a time every four years. It was all about him, sure, but that didn't matter. It didn't lessen the value of his cause. It was just. It was right. There just wasn't a need for it anymore.

He sighed in the front seat of the Range Rover.

"Oh, to be young again."

Tomorrow he would deliver the cage through the hole in the back fence. His medical bag was ready with the proper tools to bring justice to his dolls.

In the end, they thanked him. They always did. He made sure of it. If more people did what he did, there would be fewer assholes in the world. That was one of the reasons he wanted to be found out. Once everything went on record, and the newspapers wrote his story, maybe women would consider their actions. Maybe they wouldn't torment men to the point where they had to respond in anger. If he could just save a few men the pain of losing everything in a divorce, their home, their business, their kids, all because *she* cheated on him, then maybe what he did was righteous after all.

He knew it was, but the public wouldn't at first glance.

He needed to die for his message to be heard. They would have no one to crucify if he was gone. Maybe then they would only hear the message, the true message.

A plan had formed in his head. He already had two dolls in mind. He had talked to his sister. Jennifer always told him about the abusive women at the crisis center. He heard about it year after year while he waited for the leap year.

This one was shaping up to be a grand year.

He smiled, pulled the keys from the ignition, and got out of the vehicle. The chill in the air hit him immediately. He hunched his shoulders, dropped his hands in his pockets, and started for the hole in the fence.

Once he had squeezed through, he walked the fifty meters across the snow-covered grass to the side door of the warehouse that he'd already snapped the lock off. It was mid-afternoon, but he didn't worry about being seen. The hole in the fence was at the edge of the property, and behind that, a row of train tracks sat below a hill. The nearest building was hundreds of yards away on the other side of the street.

The front of the warehouse looked out onto a large parking lot and the road that led to Keele Street. Even if someone saw him from the two-story office building on the other side of the road, they wouldn't pay too much attention. He had a magnetic security sign on both front doors of the Range Rover. If anyone saw his vehicle in the area, they would assume a security company was doing routine rounds.

Once inside the side door of the warehouse, he made his way to the back of the building and down a few stairs where a large room once stored supplies. He had chosen this room for the cage.

He walked around it, scanning every square foot, ensuring it would work. The corner would hold the cage. The water was still connected. There was a sink that would help him clean up after his mannequins lost their tongues. He wasn't in need of water for drinking. His dolls weren't allowed such niceties.

No, they came here to learn, not survive.

A bird flitted in the rafters. He looked up and followed its path.

"You'll have quite a show in here soon enough," he said to the bird. "Just a few more days."

The sound of his own voice echoing softly off the metallic walls scared him. He looked around as if he was being watched.

Then someone shouted from somewhere above.

"Hello?" The distant male voice echoed throughout the warehouse.

Goosebumps rose on his arms.

"That real estate agent said nobody was supposed to be inside this building until March," he whispered to himself. He was unarmed. No knife, no scalpel, no weapon of any kind. He had never been any good with his hands. "What am I going to do?"

"Hello?" the male voice called again. "I saw you come in."

He walked to the nearest wall and leaned against it.

Did he see me?

Maybe if he stayed out of sight and let the intruder wander off, everything would work out. But he couldn't now. Since he was seen, there were three options. Option one, kill the man and be done with it. But he didn't want to. That was anti-progress. He dealt with dolls and mannequins, not men. Option two, talk to the man, convince him that everything was fine, and then he could come back and still use the facility. Or option three, talk to the man, convince him that everything was fine, and find another facility to use. Time was running out, though. Leap day was coming up quickly. He couldn't find another facility in that time.

So he decided on option two. He had to talk to the intruder. But he couldn't do it in the room he proposed to assemble the cage, so he slipped out and ran for the stairs.

"Hello?" the voice called, sounding less certain someone was here.

"Is anyone there?" the man called as he climbed the stairs two at a time.

"Over here," the intruder said.

Across the main floor, about a hundred meters away, a man wearing a shirt and tie stood between two columns.

"Are you okay?" the shirt and tie man asked. "Are you

allowed to be in here? This place has been empty for over a year."

"Security," he shouted as he walked toward the intruder.

"Security? I've never seen security come through here before."

He continued walking toward the intruder. "New buyers or someone's looking to lease the place." They were forty yards apart now. "All I know is my company got the call to do routine patrols. We walk the premises to keep any animals out and ensure there are no squatters."

He sized the man up as he drew closer. Five foot, ten inches, about one hundred and sixty pounds, no stomach protruding, but never been to a gym either. Losing his hair on top, scruff on the face, middle-aged and without a wedding ring. Unhappy, corporate blue-collar who eats pretty well and probably doesn't have a girlfriend, lonely and with a lot of male friends. Focuses too much on what other people are doing. Shouldn't have come in here because he had no idea who or what he was going to meet.

That made him stupid.

"As security for this building, I'm going to have to ask how you gained access to this warehouse."

"Through the hole in the fence by your vehicle."

"Your name?"

"Colin James."

"Like the eighties singer?"

He nodded.

"Well, I'm not going to call this in." He smiled for Colin's benefit. "But this building is off limits. Technically, you're trespassing. Let's both walk out to the hole and leave, but I'm going to have to ask you not to come back. Can you do that?"

"Uh, sure."

"The hole is being fixed the first week of March. Until then, you'll see my vehicle almost daily, but you can't come back. Another guard might not be as cool about you walking in on my days off."

Colin nodded. "I just wanted to introduce myself and let you know I work in that building across the way. I've been keeping an eye on the building since Alba Plastics and Metals closed."

He tapped Colin on the shoulder and turned to start walking toward the exit. Colin matched his step.

"We appreciate your help, but you don't have to anymore. We got this."

"I didn't get your name," Colin said.

"Bruce," he said, the fake name he always used for times like this.

"Well, Bruce, it was nice to meet you. And I'll stay away now that you guys are on the job."

He tried to think of something security-like to ask or talk about. They walked in silence across the massive floor space and then out through the side door and into the early afternoon sun.

"Any idea how that hole in the fence got to be there?" Bruce asked.

Colin smiled wide. "I was there the day the stupid punks pried the fence back. I chased them away, but they came back a couple of times. For a while, I kept coming over with a few of my fellow employees. We got the police involved."

"Good," Bruce said, knowing that the punks Colin talked of were using the hole to gain access to the premises, taking advantage of the hole he made last August and getting in trouble for it. "We don't want squatters in here. A clean-up crew is coming through next month, and then the new company takes over after that."

"Any idea who's moving into the building?" Colin asked.

"None. They don't tell us things like that."

At the fence, Colin squeezed through first and stared down at the magnetic square on the door of the Range Rover.

"CPS? Who's that?"

"Canadian Protection Services." He had ripped them off the door of a car parked at a hotel overnight over a dozen years ago. No one had ever questioned it. But now Colin frowned.

"Everything okay?" Bruce asked. "You thinking of something you want to tell me?"

The wind had died down, and the sky was cloudless. He had to squint as the bright sun reflected off all the fresh snow surrounding them.

"No, no, just thought I'd heard of them before. No big deal. Anyway, have a great day, and stay safe out there."

Colin turned away and trudged through the snow, following the fence around the property in the boot prints he had made on the way in.

I should've killed him.

It was a mistake. This year's leap day success depended on whether Colin James decided to make a return visit. It was too risky. But he had been warned off. Hopefully, he would stay away.

If he showed his face before the ultimate reset was complete, he would have to kill him. That was all there was to it.

He walked around to the driver's side and climbed in. The interior had gotten cold. He turned the engine over and waited until the heat kicked in.

To an outsider, it would appear that he was writing a report. At least, that's what cops did after visiting a building like this.

He slammed the steering wheel.

"Everything could be fucked this year because of that idiot."

He had waited four years for this moment. He had waited four years to satisfy his urges without paying any price and to teach the ones who wanted a price to be paid what that really meant.

He waited four years to reset the wrongs, and he wasn't about to let Colin James take that away from him.

"Nobody will stop me. Nobody."

He dropped the vehicle in gear and left the property, heading downtown to sign in to his day job. He had work to do and now even more planning.

He would take his first mannequin tomorrow after the cage was in place.

Tomorrow marked the last of the resets.

Tomorrow.

Chapter 12

SARAH HAD BEEN HERE before, done this before. She was past the point of fear. The good cop, bad cop was a foolish circus act when used on her, but they always tried. There had to be a cop school of manipulation where they're all taught the same thing.

She rubbed her wrists gently, the pain from the handcuffs subsiding, the bruises rising. Her tiny shirt had dirt on it where she had been shoved onto the massage parlor's floor. Residue from the cop's boots had smeared on her breasts and stomach. It had dried, but smudges of dirt remained.

What charges were they going to threaten her with this time? With her reputation and a trio of cops coming to her home the previous night asking for her help, she didn't think anything would stick. This was routine. This was their process, but it was all bullshit.

The door to the small interrogation room opened, and

two men dressed in suits stepped inside, then closed the door.

"Do you want a lawyer present?" the taller one asked while the short one walked to the corner and leaned against the wall.

"No need for one," Sarah said.

The tall one dropped a folder on the table. "You're being charged with many offenses, two of which are attempted murder and uttering death threats. That puts you in the system for the next year. Attempted murder is pretty serious, so you may be stuck here for several years rotting in a prison cell."

"Really?" she asked. "Is that how assholes do it in Canada?"

The two men exchanged glances.

"Excuse me? We have the sworn statement of the woman who was in the kitchen of the massage parlor with you. She said …" He picked up the file, flipped through a few pages, and stopped, tracking something with his finger. "Ah, here it is. She said your words were, 'I'm going to put five more bullets in your face.'" He closed the file and dropped it on the table. "She went on to say that you described where each bullet would enter his face in detail. Is that true?"

Sarah nodded. "Absolutely true."

They exchanged another glance. "You don't deny it?"

"No. He deserved it. But I didn't shoot him." She shrugged and looked down at the table. "Maybe next time."

"Ohhh," he laughed. "There won't be a next time—"

"Would you shut up?" Sarah said.

"Excuse me."

She met his gaze with a cold stare. "I told you to shut up. You're wasting your time telling me about the charges I'm going to have to endure for years. If that's the case, where's my arraignment, my bail hearing? I haven't even been read my rights. You fucking amateurs. Get me somebody who really wants to talk to me."

He looked stunned but did his best to cover it up. "Do you realize the trouble you're in?"

"Oh, no," she said in a scared voice. She wrapped her arms around her shoulders and shivered. "You're right. I am in trouble. Now fuck off and bring in the man who's pulling your strings. I'm done talking to the puppet."

The tall one stood open-mouthed and stared at her. After a few seconds, the other man pushed off the wall. On his way to the door, he tugged on his partner's sleeve, and they exited together.

Not more than five minutes passed before the door opened again, and Alan Lyson, the man from her apartment last night, walked in alone. He took the chair across the table from her and sat down.

"Miss Roberts."

"Lyson."

"You really upset some people around here with your antics."

"You want to talk about upset? You want to piss me off?"

"No, of course not."

"A man walked into that massage parlor and shot Rita without provocation. I ran that beaten-down woman into the kitchen and barred the door. The perp threatened to shoot the door down. Take a look. The door's a piece of balsa wood. He would've gotten through it within seconds, and we'd both be dead. I opened the door, allowed him entry, and gave him a flesh wound. Once his weapon was secure, I got the wound tied off. Then I came out with my hands in the air. Everything was by the book. Your asshole brotherhood in fucking blue," she smacked the table hard, making Lyson jump, "attacked me and nearly broke my wrists and dislocated my shoulders. They called me a slut and a whore. I want their fucking badges for that. Do you hear me?"

Lyson nodded. He appeared afraid to say anything.

She calmed a little before attempting to talk again. "If you know anything about me, you will know why I was there today. You will know that I was directed to be there to save that girl's life."

He nodded.

"I wore this," she gestured at her dirty shirt that showed all her cleavage, "to gain access to the premises because they have that buzzer system. I needed to be inside to save her. Get it?"

He nodded again.

"Can you do anything other than nod?"

His head stopped moving. "The officers who responded to the call said you walked up the hall with the gun on your person."

"Yes, okay, probably a stupid move in hindsight, but I'm not leaving that gun behind. It's too important to me. I didn't leave it in that warehouse in Vegas, and I'm not leaving it here."

"Warehouse in Vegas?"

"Don't worry about it. Long story."

"Are you interested in hearing me out?"

"Do I have a choice?"

"I could hold you for twenty-four hours without charging you or charge you based on that women's statement and keep you longer. But I don't want to do that."

"You mean to tell me she actually gave a statement that I wanted to kill that guy?"

He nodded, then caught himself and said, "Yes."

"That bitch. Sometimes saving people isn't what it's all cracked up to be."

"I'm a cop near retirement. I know exactly what you're saying."

She dropped her hands to her thighs, squared her shoulders, and said, "Go ahead then. Tell me what it is you've got to say. Then I'm leaving."

The door opened, and another man entered. He was a husky man with thick shoulders, slicked-back hair, and black-rimmed glasses. He held a large file.

"Just put that here," Lyson said.

The man did as he was told and moved to the door. He closed it, staying inside the room, and leaned on it.

"That's Justin Ferman. He's one of the members on the task force that was put together in the last couple of days to deal with all the bodies." Lyson opened the file in front of him.

"All the bodies?" Sarah echoed.

"Yeah. So far, we've located six dead women with their tongues removed. They were found in homemade cages. One was wrapped neatly in a garbage bag. The MO is definitely the same in each case. We're hoping you can help us find the killer before he strikes again."

It was her turn to be stunned. "How do you know he will strike again?"

"Because it'll be February 29th in a few days."

"What's the leap year have to do with dead bodies? Or

future dead bodies, for that matter?"

"We received a letter from the killer three days ago outlining what he had been doing on each leap year and where to find the bodies of his victims. He's being called The Leap Year Killer, and we intend to stop him." He paused. "With your help, of course."

Chapter 13

HE SURVEYED THE CAGE, opening and closing the door to ensure it fit just right. The lock engaged, then disengaged properly.

He had entered the warehouse after dark when the business across the street closed, and everyone had gone home. Staking the company out from up the street had proven easy. For the task of bringing the cage walls in, he had rented a small cube van, and he'd left the magnetic security advertisements off the vehicle. This part of the industrial neighborhood was empty by nine in the evening. He backed the truck up as close as possible and dressed all in black. He loaded as much as possible onto a flat wooden toboggan and dragged the cage walls to the broken fence and into the building.

Now that it was assembled, it stood four feet tall. It was long enough for a six-foot woman to lie down or sit cross-legged. Having two in there made it a little cramped, but this wasn't here for comfort.

He checked his medical bag to ensure everything was in place for what he needed to do when his first woman arrived tomorrow night. He would have to spend a lot of time dealing with her over the week in case Colin James returned. Discovering what he was up to before leap day would thwart his plans.

The timers for the explosives were set, and the explosives were in place.

His plan had changed. The letter he had anonymously left at the police station with Alan Lyson's name on it had been perfect. He was surprised that the newspapers hadn't printed anything on their findings yet, but he knew they had all six bodies of his previous victims. He had seen the bodies himself as they came in.

But he wasn't in charge of press releases and wasn't being told when that would occur.

So in the meantime, he would continue with his plans, finish with his last two dolls and then destroy the evidence in a grand fashion.

He had learned of the eleven most popular explosive components insurgents used in their bombs, which included ammonium nitrate, potassium chlorate, nitrocellulose, RDX, and C-4.

Because he knew someone who could put him in contact with someone who sold C-4, there was enough C-4 in six different places throughout the warehouse to take the entire building down.

They were hidden so well that only bomb-sniffing dogs could find them. A crack in the floor at a random corner.

Underneath the ridge of the stairs and covered in a black cloth. Because no one would expect to be looking for bombs, they would never be found. The timers were set for just before midnight, February 29.

His line of work also enabled him to learn how to build the cage himself. He had seen a cage like this on a case over fifteen years ago and had been fascinated by it. If the task force investigated how he procured his materials and hid his victims and what cages he used, if they really looked deep at his methods, they would discover the root was the criminal element already out there, schooling him from his exposure to the police station in downtown Toronto.

He set up a Bunsen burner and placed the scalpel on the table beside it. He would need to operate on his victim as soon as she arrived while the doll was still drugged.

He walked to the corner and switched off the portable lights. Then he turned on his flashlight and slowly walked through the warehouse basement. As he neared the top of the stairs, he closed his eyes tight and turned the flashlight off.

After half a minute of standing still and listening to the empty warehouse, he opened his eyes, hoping they had adjusted to the darkness enough to see his way out without the flashlight.

He stumbled a few times but made it to the side door and then hopped outside onto the snow. The toboggan was where he had left it. After dragging it across the snow, he tossed it in the back of the truck and drove away, not turning on the headlights until he was two blocks south on Keele Street.

Half an hour later, he pulled over on a random street and dumped the toboggan in front of a house. Maybe some kid would discover it and take it home.

Then he drove the truck back, dropped the keys in the slot at the rental company's office door, and hopped in his cold Range Rover.

It was time to go home and rest. After work tomorrow, he needed to pay a visit to Janice Weston at the strip club where she worked as a whore. He had his chloroform and napkin ready and a life lesson for her on his agenda. He knew exactly how much chloroform to administer to his doll so she wouldn't die from it. He couldn't have that. Death would happen on his terms.

When chloroform was first discovered in the early 1800s, they used it as an anesthetic while women gave birth. He knew how powerful it could be and, used properly, how beneficial it was.

He was kind enough to use it while removing their tongues.

No one should be awake for that.

He started the engine and drove home, so happy with his success that he even listened to the radio and tried to sing along.

He hadn't done that since he was a teenager and idealistic.

Oh, how the world had changed.

Chapter 14

Sarah got up from her chair and moved to the side of the interrogation room. "What the hell are you talking about?" she asked. "How many bodies again? And explain the letter, too."

"Okay," Lyson said. "I'll start at the beginning."

"Please do."

"But first, let's move to a more comfortable office."

"And coffee?" Sarah asked. "I'll need coffee for this. Or something stronger. Got whiskey?"

"Coffee."

"Fine."

Sarah headed for the door at the same time Lyson did. The husky man had already opened it and disappeared down the hall.

"Am I still being charged with anything?" Sarah asked.

Lyson stopped at the door. He smiled down at her. "Don't

be mad at me."

"Don't fuck around, and I won't be mad."

"There's a camera in the lobby of the massage parlor and one in the kitchen. They aren't supposed to record audio, but the woman running the joint did anyway. I watched the whole thing go down ten minutes before I entered this room. You did what I would've done. There won't be any charges."

"Okay, I'm not mad about that. I'm relieved, actually. Because you saw the conduct of those idiots who arrested me. What happens to those asshole cops who called me slut and whore? Do I get them alone in a room for five minutes?"

"No. As much as I'd love to watch that, all three have been suspended with pay and are going in for sensitivity training. But the gun in your pants wasn't cool."

She raised her eyebrows. "I'm not leaving it behind. It means a lot. Which reminds me, when do I get it back?"

"When you leave today."

"Fine. But don't let me see any of those three assholes. I'm warning you. I won't be able to control my temper. When I look at them, I don't see police officers, only pigs with dirty mouths who need them washed out with the heel of my foot."

"Usually, it's the other way around."

"What?"

"You know, the cop and pig comment."

"You said it, not me." She shrugged.

Lyson led the way out to the stairs. Minutes later, they entered a conference room with a long table and a dozen chairs.

"I remember this room," Sarah said. "Detective Waller announced his retirement to us in here last summer."

"I heard about that."

She took a seat while Lyson walked to the side table where he turned on a Mr. Coffee machine. Without her cell phone, she had no idea if Aaron had been trying to get a hold of her. He was probably still at the dojo, but if he had called, he would be worried by now. Then he would leave work in an attempt to locate her. She hated the idea of checking in. It was foreign to her, something she'd never had to do before, but that was part of being in a relationship.

"I've got to call Aaron."

Lyson looked at her over his shoulder. "Phone's over there." He gestured to a small table by the window.

Sarah slid her chair over and picked the phone up. She dialed the dojo and got one of Aaron's teachers, Daniel.

"Hi. Aaron around?"

"Hey, Sarah. No, he left half an hour ago. Something about you."

"Me?"

"Yeah. He couldn't reach you."

"Shit."

"Everything okay?"

"Yeah. Just call him on his cell and tell him I'm fine."

"Can he call your cell?"

"It's at home."

"And you're not … okay. I'll tell him."

"Thanks, Daniel."

"No problem. Ciao."

Sarah hung up and slid the chair back to the table as Lyson set the coffees down.

"Didn't know what you took in your coffee. Cream and sugar are over there."

"It's fine like this."

The door opened, and Justin, the husky guy from the interrogation room, stepped inside. He took a chair opposite Sarah.

She nodded at him. He nodded back.

"I won't promise anything," she said. "I told you last night that I don't work with anybody, and generally, I don't trust the police."

"I know, and after what happened today, I understand. But you're already connected to this case."

That perked her up. "How so?"

"I'll get to that."

"No, you will not. Tell me how I'm connected, or I un-connect myself and walk out that door. Good luck finding me after that."

"Damn, you're direct," Lyson said.

Justin sat forward on his chair. "The crisis center," he said.

"What about it?"

"You were there yesterday."

"And?"

"We've identified the bodies—"

"Already? That was fast."

"Each body had ID just outside the cage they died in. Their killer wanted us to know who they were right away."

"And you're sure it all matches?" Sarah asked.

"No, but the medical examiner …" Justin stopped and flipped a couple of pages back in the file he held. "Martin Rankin will do his best to confirm they match the ID left behind."

She blew on her coffee and took a sip. A moment of silence fell over them. Sarah broke it with another question.

"You were saying how I was connected."

"According to the IDs found at the scenes, all six women have missing persons files that are cold cases. Over the last few days, we've examined as much as possible about women's lives, looking for something in common. We need to determine how all six could've met their murderer or were they picked up randomly."

"Okay, and did you find anything yet?"

"All six were with abusive boyfriends. Only one was married."

Sarah looked at Lyson. "Does he always take this long to tell a story?" She turned to Justin before Lyson could respond. "Hurry and tell me how I'm connected."

"They had all visited the same crisis center you were at yesterday within days of the missing persons report being filed. You were there yesterday, but those injuries you have are healed."

Lyson cut in. "The broken nose happened in Vegas. I suspected as much, but now I know because I called down there. Also, Aaron isn't into abusing women. Not from the case that hit the courts a while back when he was charged with attempted murder. The man he beat was one of his students who had beaten up his own daughter. Aaron lost his sister and almost died trying to find justice for her. He's no abuser." Lyson tapped a pen on the table. "So, tell us, why did you show up at the crisis center yesterday and lie about someone abusing you?"

"I have no idea."

Chapter 15

Special Agent Penn Kierian tapped on the car window. Clint started and turned the radio down.

"Anything happening?" Kierian asked.

"No. Aaron left for work at his usual time. He showed up ten minutes ago, but I haven't seen Sarah all day."

"What? Why would he come home? It's the middle of the day?"

"I have no idea. Didn't think about it. Sarah's our target."

Kierian looked up and down the street. The weather had broken, and today was bright and sunny even though the sun was already going down. More people were out and about today, the street busier.

"Hey," Clint said. "You think this surveillance of Sarah will end soon, and we can go home? I mean, what are we doing this for anyway?"

"You know why we're doing this. Don't ask such stupid

questions. We go home and take Sarah with us once she performs one of her tricks. The closer we study her, the sooner we see the psychic stuff."

Clint opened the car door and got out to stand beside Kierian. "What's bothering you?"

"After those cops talked to her last night, I don't know. I just have a funny feeling something's going on."

"Like what?" Clint started picking at something in his teeth.

"Never mind. Are you sure Sarah is in the apartment?"

"I didn't see her leave. That's all I'm sure of."

Kierian pulled out his cell phone and started dialing.

"Who you calling?" Clint asked.

"Aaron."

"Aaron? Why?"

Kierian didn't answer as the phone in Aaron's apartment began ringing.

"Sarah?" Aaron answered.

"Is she at home?" Kierian asked, but he already knew the answer.

"Who's calling?"

He ended the call. "Shit. She's gone, and Aaron came home looking for her."

"How did you get all that?"

"Because of the way he answered the phone. He had hoped it would be her."

Clint spun in a slow circle. "Where could she be?"

"I have no idea, but we're tasked to follow one girl and fucking that up—" he stopped. "Oh no ..."

"What?" Clint asked.

"She's probably with those cops again." He pushed Clint

out of the way and hopped in the driver's seat. "Get in. We're going downtown."

He started the engine and hit the gas as soon as Clint dropped in the other side of the car.

"Call our boss. If she's downtown, have someone of authority pull those men off Sarah. If you have to, talk to the chief of police again."

"What if they don't have her? We're going to look like idiots."

"Just make the call. You fucked this up. Now fix it."

Clint dialed and held the phone to his ear. "And if they don't have her?" he asked again.

"Make the call!" Kierian shouted as he ran a red light, using his horn as a warning.

Chapter 16

HE FOLLOWED THE TAXI to the strip club on The Queensway in Mississauga and watched Janice enter the front door for her evening shift. Since the day of the taking was upon him, his urges were loose, and he anticipated having her in the cage. It was his time again, and the reset was upon them.

Steering his Range Rover toward the back of the building, he parked close to the door where the girls came outside for smoke breaks. Ontario's strict smoking laws ensured the ladies had to smoke outside, even in winter. They had a little picnic table by the door, cleared of snow, where the girls chatted and used a large coffee can as their ashtray.

It was late afternoon or early evening. He had spent the day dealing with the bodies of his other six victims, helping with the investigation, making points, and guessing right. At least as far as his colleagues understood. He looked brilliant. But now he had the rest of the evening off. He would report to work for two more days, filing everything properly in case it went to court one day, even though he knew it never would.

It will never go to court if I'm dead.

Then he would leave his last letter requesting Alan Lyson and that pesky intruder, Sarah Roberts, to meet him at the warehouse alone at 23:55hrs on February 29. He wouldn't be there if they didn't come alone, and they would never solve this case. When his explosives detonated at midnight, he would have his moment.

He settled back into his seat for the long wait. Since Janice had just reported for work, she wouldn't take a smoke break immediately.

He decided to go in and have a drink.

Without thinking any more about it, he left his vehicle and headed for the front door of the club. The music thumped and pounded even before he opened the door. As he stepped inside the club, a woman's voice sang through the speakers about putting a ring on it. A bouncer greeted him with a nod. Getting seen in a place like this, especially the night one of the club's girls was about to go missing, was not in his playbook. But since this was his last play, it didn't matter.

He entered the main area. Purple lights were suspended above the stage in the otherwise darkened club. Small tables were scattered about the carpeted floor. Beer-drinking men randomly sat among them. Women in various states of undress walked around chatting with the men, no doubt asking if they wanted a dance. A couple of women sat and drank with potential customers. One dancer walked a man toward the VIP sign in the back, pulling him along by the hand.

None of the girls were Janice.

He moved farther into the club and sat at a table at least two away from anyone else. A waitress came by and said something, but he couldn't hear her over the music.

"A Bud, please," he shouted back, and the waitress walked away.

Before he got his drink, a dancer wearing a see-through bra and a very small lace thong approached him from the other side of the cavernous room. She took the seat beside him and smiled.

She was wiry thin, and her eyes were rimmed with the effects of drug use. What the officers on the street called a 'meth diet.' He wanted to tell her that he didn't offer her a seat. He wanted to tell her to fuck off, that he didn't pay for pussy. He had a litany of words rise to his tongue, but in the end, he remained silent.

"You wanna dance, Honey?" she yelled over the music.

The Budweiser dropped in over his shoulder. He heard the waitress ask for the money because she was so close to his ear. He paid, and she walked away.

The dancer didn't move. He took a long swig of his beer and set it back down on the table, surveying the crowd, looking for his subject.

"So how about it?" the woman asked again, edging closer, her knee touching his.

He pulled his knee away and glared at her. She gave him a dirty look and got up.

Next time, don't sit unless you're invited.

He drank his beer, worried that he still couldn't see his subject.

His sister had told him about her. At the crisis center, this woman had explained that she was being a bitch to her boyfriend, and he'd hit her. They lived together, but she wanted to know if the crisis center could arrange for a new apartment. When Jennifer had asked what made her think she deserved such violence, she had talked about all the men she had had sex with from the club where she worked. In the VIP lounge, for the right price, she had started doing anything the customer wanted. It was frowned upon, but the money was too good to stop. Then she started enjoying her job more.

Her boyfriend had suspicions. He'd sent a friend in to offer her five hundred dollars. They had sex in the back booth, and she went home to a violent and upset boyfriend. It was time for her to leave him, and that was why she had gone to the crisis center.

Because of her income, even though most of it wasn't declared, and her overall situation, the center couldn't help her with housing but offered counseling and other options to ease her out of the life she was living. She refused, yelled at Jennifer that she didn't know what her life was like, and stormed out.

Jennifer doesn't know what life is like?

He chuckled and sipped his beer.

He recently found out from Jennifer that the crisis center had helped 1,144 rape victims last year alone, 320 of those under the age of eighteen and half of those under thirteen. Crisis centers did a good thing wherever they were. Jennifer knew what life was all about and how tragic life could be. She lived it every day when the shell-shocked faces of the raped entered her office.

Jennifer had told him about it over the phone two weeks ago, and that was when he decided this woman needed to learn the consequences of her actions. He was prepared to make her accountable.

It was one thing when a woman was beaten up or raped for no reason. But when she asked for it and then tried to get the guy in trouble when she had it coming—that was where he drew the line.

Janice had to pay for what she did.

And for what she does to men in that VIP lounge.

He drank from his beer again, which was half empty. His stomach turned at the thought of missing her. Could she have shown up to quit and left already? Could he have missed her when he parked at the back by the smoking area?

When he finished his drink, he planned to return to his vehicle and wait out there. She would either show, or he would have to come back another night.

The girl on stage was too skinny. She appeared to be either drunk or stoned, as her movements were uncoordinated. She swung around the pole too many times, holding on with her right hand, swaying to and fro to a Led Zeppelin classic.

On his last pull from the bottle, his subject stepped onto the floor. Janice had been in the VIP lounge all this time. A man came out behind her, tucking his shirt in.

"You little bitch," he whispered, not afraid anyone would hear over the music. "You're the one who has a price to pay."

He'd seen enough. He had played it cool this long. Watching his subject take man after man back to VIP might make him grab her in the middle of the club. Then he would have to deal with the bouncers, and he wouldn't be able to go to work tomorrow, and everything would be blown, and he …

He smacked his face hard.

"Enough!" he scolded himself.

A man three tables over, turned to him, met his eyes, and then glanced away.

He got to his feet and started across the carpeted club floor without looking at his subject again. He would see her soon enough. He passed the bouncer, smacked the door hard on the way out, and took a deep breath of the cold air. The temperature was dropping. Cars raced by on The Queensway, oblivious of who he was and what he was about to do.

Maybe it is better that way. The public lives in bliss, not knowing who I really am and that I live among them. Fucking ignorant ants.

He jumped off the steps and walked through the parking lot toward his vehicle. As he neared it, two women were smoking by the picnic table. He had to get closer to see if one of them was his subject.

One of the girls was a short-haired blonde with a thick fur coat covering her shoulders. Janice had long brown hair like the other woman who stood with her back to him. She wore a black winter coat, but Janice had worn a red winter coat to work.

He got to about even with them, his Range Rover two vehicles up. Then he turned at the same time the woman with the long brown hair turned toward him.

It was her. His subject. Janice.

This was his chance. He needed the chloroform. And he needed to deal with the other woman.

He reached his car, opened the door, and pulled the chloroform cloth out. The bottle had the right amount, measured previously, and he dabbed it onto the cloth.

He shut the door and popped open the tailgate as he

glanced at the picnic table. Both women were still there, but their cigarettes were almost done.

Leaving his tailgate open, he walked toward them.

"Excuse me?" he called from just a few feet away. Their faces said this was their private time. Talk to them inside, or don't talk to them at all.

Yeah, well, fuck you both.

"I wonder if either of you could help me locate Dundas Street. I think it's around here somewhere." He came prepared with a small map that he pulled out of his pocket, unfolding it as he did. "Is it close?"

Music thumped behind the back door, which sat propped open with a broom handle. He stepped in closer and opened the map for them to look at while scanning the immediate area.

No one was in the parking lot. This was a perfect time.

But what should he do with the second girl?

It was now or never.

"It's not far," his subject answered without looking down at the map. "Just take The Queensway that way." She gestured west.

Before she could turn back around, he stumbled over his feet on purpose, tripped close to the back door, and jammed his foot onto the tip of the broom handle, forcing it deep into the back of the club. It slid inside perfectly, and the door closed, latching with an audible click.

He collected himself and turned around. "I'm so sorry, ladies."

Disgust showed on both their faces.

"Why'd you do that?" the short-haired girl asked. "Shit, now we have to walk all the way around to the front. Way to go, Moe." She dropped her cigarette to the wet pavement and stomped on it, twisting her foot as if to drive it into the ground.

He chuckled. "Moe? You've got to be kidding."

The girls looked at each other, clearly wanting him gone. This was their private break area. He didn't belong.

As fast as he could, he pulled the chloroform napkin out of his pocket and jammed it onto Janice's face. She grunted and yanked her head back but banged into the brick wall behind her. She clawed at his forearm with both hands, which he had expected, but it would only be another second or two before she was asleep.

The short-haired woman had moved behind him. He knew he needed to keep an eye on her. What if she ran? Memorized his license plate number? For a brief second, he realized how stupid and risky this was.

Then all thoughts left his mind as a sudden and sharp pain rose from his groin. He looked down just as his feet settled onto the concrete again. The short-haired woman's hand was squeezing his scrotum from behind as she screamed. She held on at a steady rate of strength, but things were numbing for him below the waist.

"Let her go!" she yelled, but it didn't matter anymore. When she had grabbed him, both his hands had shot upward, removing the napkin from Janice's face.

Janice lay on the wet concrete, unconscious. He had done it, and if he had one clear thought through all the pain he felt, he knew he had to neutralize the other woman too, or he would be in jail before the night was over.

Ignoring the pain as much as he could, he shouted an animalistic cry, twisted his upper body around, and bent down toward the other woman, jamming the chloroform napkin onto her face. She pulled back and away, trying in vain to get away from his probing hand. In doing so, her hand released his scrotum.

He dropped to his knees with a loud grunt, never letting his hand fall from her face. She was a fighter, writhing under his grip while backing away on her butt. In the end, he held on long enough, and there was plenty of chloroform to make her lose consciousness, too.

Exhausted, spent, and in a great deal of pain, he lay there for a few heartbeats and just breathed. Time was running out. Someone else could pop out the door for a smoke break or check on the shouting. A customer could happen upon them.

He pushed himself up to a sitting position, looked around, and then got to his feet. He forced one leg in front of the other even though he wanted to lie down and wait for the pain to subside. His legs obliged him as long as he spread them wide with each step, careful not to brush up against his scrotum.

She would pay for what she did to him. He had to pay, so she would, too.

Janice was light. Getting her into the back of the Range Rover proved easy. He dropped her in roughly as a car drove by, looking for a parking spot. He waited until the vehicle had passed and then went back for the second girl.

Getting her inside the back of the Rover was tougher, and he considered himself lucky that no one came out the back door the entire time. He shut and secured his gate, then hopped around to the driver's side and jumped in.

He had done it and got more than he bargained for—two bad women for the price of one.

Signs like this proved what he did was righteous. If he weren't supposed to be fixing things, resetting the wrongs they had perpetrated, then someone would've interrupted him.

He started the vehicle, left the parking lot, and got onto Highway 427, heading north. Once on Keele Street, he kept to the speed of traffic. When he pulled onto the street with the warehouse and his homemade cage, only the streetlights shone. The buildings were all dark.

Neither woman woke during the twenty-minute ride. He killed his lights and rolled to a stop near the toboggan tracks from earlier. Behind the front seat, the magnetic strips advertising the security firm sat where he had placed them. Once they were affixed to each door, he checked on his captives. Both were still deep in a drugged sleep.

To ensure they didn't wake until he was ready, he opened another bottle of chloroform, dabbed a new cloth with it, and held it over each girl's nose for a few quick moments.

"There, that should do it."

The far-off traffic was the only noise at this time of night. In this part of the industrial community at this hour, there wouldn't be too much traffic close by. Even if a vehicle happened upon his Range Rover, the security signs wouldn't garner a second glance.

He pulled the feisty one out first and dragged her by her heels through the snow, through the hole in the fence, and then into the building's side door. Once in the warehouse, he pulled her up and onto his shoulder fireman style and walked her downstairs to the cage. Minutes later, she was lying on her back in the cage, still sleeping. He checked her pulse. Steady and regular.

His scrotum felt better, which made him lighter on his feet. He hustled back outside and found Janice sleeping peacefully in the Rover.

After pulling her out and getting her inside, he shut the side door, lifted her up, and carried her to the basement room, but he didn't put her in the cage right away. She needed her operation while she was still unconscious.

I'm humane. I won't slice your tongue off and suture it while you're awake.

Smiling at his kindness, he laid her down on the floor on her back. Then he removed her jacket, halter top, and mini-skirt. Once she was completely naked, he admired her body. Any man willing to pay the price could have such a thing of perfection. Because of that, it was her turn to pay the price.

He rubbed his hands along her tanned skin, stopping on her nipples to caress them.

"When you wake, we'll have more fun. Don't get me wrong. I don't mind doing everything while you're drugged and sleeping—actually, that's preferred. I hate the protests and the crying. But you get a reprieve the first night because my ball sac is just too sore. Sadly, that bitch over there ruined our first evening together."

He got up, walked over to the medical bag, and removed the scalpel. Then he held it over the flame of the Bunsen burner.

"When the scalpel is hot like this, it helps to cauterize the tongue and limits bleeding," he explained to his unconscious victim. "After that, I'll use a cautery unit to burn the open cut, closing off blood vessels, which prevents further bleeding." He turned to her with the hot scalpel ready in his hand. "But what do you care? You'll sleep through the entire thing. When you wake tomorrow, we'll be ready to have fun."

He knelt beside her and ran a hand along her perfect thigh, stopping on the edge of her vagina.

"Oh, the fun we'll have this week."

Then he forced her mouth open. Using a clamp, he grabbed the tip of her pink tongue and pulled it out as far as possible.

With the scalpel as hot as it was, the edge cut into the base of her tongue easily.

He laughed as he sliced, knowing he was doing the work he was supposed to be doing.

The ultimate reset had begun, and he was the man to finish it.

Chapter 17

KIERIAN AND CLINT MADE it to the police station downtown, hopped out of the Impala, and ran inside. Clint had gathered that the Toronto police were processing Sarah Roberts for something. Their contact in the States hadn't learned any more in such a short time. The chief of police was being called and asked to cooperate again.

Kierian wondered what the chief was being told to get his cooperation so readily. Still, he figured it was something like national security or Sarah was under the protection of the United States. In the end, it didn't matter as long as the Toronto police backed off. They had a mission. Even though it had gone on many more months than anticipated, and he was feeling as lazy about it as Clint was, they still had to see it through.

Had they caught up with her in Vegas, they could've offered her the deal. But without recent proof of her capabilities, the deal remained off the table.

They reached the front desk together.

Kierian held his FBI credentials up for the officer to see. "We understand Sarah Roberts, an American citizen, is being processed here."

"FBI, eh?" He studied the badge and looked back at Kierian. "I'll take a look."

The officer turned to his computer and typed on the keyboard. After a minute, he turned back.

"There's no Sarah Roberts in our system. Sorry guys. You'll have to look elsewhere—"

"She's in there. Check again."

The cop's face hardened. "I just checked. She ain't in there."

"Check again," Kierian said. "She is."

He mumbled something unintelligible to himself and leaned back in his chair, crossing his arms.

"What are you doing?" Kierian asked. "Where is Sarah Roberts? We have to speak to her."

"I have no idea. If she were here, I could tell you. But she ain't."

Kierian's tolerance for asshole cops dropped to an all-new low. "Then put me through to the Chief of Police. Tell him Special Agent Kierian of the FBI is here, and we need to talk."

The cop chuckled. "Yeah, right. I'll just dial him up and get him on the line for you." He spoke in a high-pitched teenaged voice, mocking Kierian.

Clint's phone chimed. They stepped back from the counter as Clint answered it. The reprieve came at the right time. Kierian was close to reaching across the desk and strangling the self-righteous asshole.

After a couple of mumbled comments, Clint extended his phone to the cop behind the desk, who refused to take it.

Clint pulled his phone back and hit a button on it. "You're on speaker, sir. Go ahead."

"This is Chief Jones," he said. "Offer these men your full cooperation. An American citizen named Sarah Roberts is under their observation. If she is in the building, locate her. These men need to speak with her. Is that understood?"

"Yes, sir," the Toronto cop said. He sat up in front of his computer and typed furiously.

"Thank you, sir," Clint said into the phone and clicked off speaker. Then he ended the call.

"She's in interrogation room four downstairs."

"Is there a lawyer present?" Kierian asked.

The cop shrugged. "I have no idea. But I'll have someone escort you two down there immediately."

How fast the tone changes ...

Chapter 18

AARON STOOD AT THE living room window, looking out at the cold evening. Sarah could be anywhere.

The phone rang again. This time Aaron picked it up and didn't say Sarah's name. He didn't say a thing. He just listened.

"Is anyone there?" a man asked.

"Who's this?"

"I need to speak with Sarah Roberts."

"Yeah, sure. No problem. But not until I know who you are."

There was a pause at the other end. "I don't give out my name freely. I prefer anonymity."

"Think of me as the gatekeeper. The key to getting past me is a name. That's all. No name, no Sarah."

The man cleared his throat. "Who are you?"

"My name is Aaron Stevens. You called my home."

"The apartment on the second floor, downtown? Walking distance to your gym?"

"How do you know all that?"

"Penny told me."

"Penny? Who's that? And stop talking in circles."

"Penny was my daughter."

"*Was* your daughter? Then how could she tell you—wait, I don't know any Penny. How would Penny know me?"

More silence on the line. Something Sarah had told him came to mind.

"Are you Sarah's cousin?" Aaron asked.

"Yes," he said as if he breathed the word out.

"Russell? It's been a while."

"Please don't say my name."

"Why call now? What's happening?"

"Sarah, please."

"She's not here."

"Where is she?" He sounded desperate. "Should I call back?"

"I have no idea where she is. Why?"

"I have to warn her."

"Warn her? And stop with the circles. Just tell me what you have to say."

"Penny told me …" He sobbed through the phone. "That Sarah wouldn't make it."

"What are you talking about?" Aaron's anger rose. "That sounds like a threat. Sarah always makes it."

"Not this time. I was told it would be fire or a bomb. She has no choice this time. She will comply because that's who she is. Her own stubbornness will kill her. Her own desire to help will be her downfall. Sarah will die in a week if she doesn't stop now."

"There has to be a way," Aaron shouted. "I'll stop her."

"It's already done. Nothing can stop it. But …"

"What?"

"If for some reason she makes it, tell her I'll see her at the hotel. Don't worry. I'll be there. I'll check in a few days before."

"What hotel? What the hell are you talking about?"

"I don't know yet."

"Is this how you always talk? This is so confusing."

"You're telling me."

"How can you help if you don't know what's going on yourself?"

"I'm in Toronto to help a family member. Sarah knows this. Sarah is my family. So I will help even though I don't want to get involved. But this time, I get to see my daughter."

"I thought Sarah said your daughter was murdered?"

The line went dead.

Chapter 19

A WOMAN ENTERED THE conference room as Sarah was about to explain how Vivian worked, even though she was sure Lyson already knew.

"This is Maria Stone, also on the task force," Lyson said. He turned to her. "Is there something new?"

"I just wanted to be here for the debriefing. Clear up any loose ends."

"Step in whenever you want."

Sarah touched her coffee mug, but it was cold, and she didn't want another. Her stomach turned at what Vivian had gotten her involved in. This seemed bigger than before. Vivian was good at saving people from accidents, stopping a kidnapping, or keeping Sarah away from would-be murderers. Tying Sarah into an active murder investigation of an active serial killer was something new.

"Lyson?" Sarah said. "You know what I do? You looked

me up, right?"

"I did." He nodded.

Maria walked around the end of the table and sat in the chair beside Sarah, clasping her hands on the table in front of her.

"Are you aware of how I do what I do?"

"I understand you're an automatic writer. Is that what they call it?"

Sarah nodded.

"Like a psychic?" Maria asked.

"Yes, but what I do is unique, different."

"How so?"

"The messages given to me through the use of my arm, my body, are about future crimes or accidents. People who aren't supposed to die or get hurt. I'm told when it'll happen and sometimes how to stop it. All I do is show up and keep to the message details as best as I can. I'm virtually assured success if I can do that."

"Is a broken nose success? Bullet holes? Knife wounds?"

"Mistakes on my part. I chose to walk back into a warehouse to get my gun. It almost killed me. Vivian had nothing to do with that. Although, in the end, leaving my gun behind was what saved me."

"What are the messages telling you to do in Toronto?"

"None of your business."

Lyson set his pen down, looked at his task force members Justin and Maria, and then back at Sarah, his face stern.

"I'm not following. Why tell us all this and then not tell us what the messages say? You were in the crisis center. You were at the massage parlor where you saved a girl's life. Where you go next and what you're supposed to do could break our case. What if you're supposed to stop a man from taking a girl? He could be our Leap Year Killer. So you need to tell us. What's next?"

Sarah pushed her chair out and walked to the window. A fresh layer of snow covered Toronto from the wintery day before.

"I heard once that a man named Mel was the mayor of Toronto."

"He was. Mel Lastman. What about him?"

"Didn't he bring in the army to clear the streets of Toronto after a big storm once? Got some flak for it? Even though he put the people of Toronto first?"

"That's him."

"Before I agree to tell you my plans for the next few days and before I ask my sister to see if she could help, tell me all you've got. Give me the snowstorm. I'll see if the army can help."

"Interesting way to put it."

"I don't want to seem disrespectful. I know the role you all play, and I do respect it. People are safe and asleep at night in their beds because of people like you. My hat's off to you for that. But I've had a rough go with cops and authorities in general. I don't trust them." She turned from the window and searched the faces of the task force members. "I've learned to keep Vivian's messages to myself, deal with each one and move on as best as possible. I want a life, too. I didn't ask for this. My conscience bought it. Now I pay for it. I'm duty-bound. Now it's an honor to serve. The only people who ever give me a hard time are the authorities. So understand, my first answer is no. Convince me otherwise."

"Fair enough," Lyson said. "I appreciate you being candid with us. Let's start at the beginning. Maria?"

She unclasped her hands and brushed her hair over her shoulders. Sarah yearned to change out of the cleavage-baring shirt and wondered how any of them took her seriously while she still wore it. Neither Lyson nor Justin had checked out her breasts yet. At least not as far as she could tell. They had been professional throughout the meeting.

Maria cleared her throat. "We have six female Caucasians. Two from four years ago, two from eight, and two from twelve years ago. One of the two from twelve years ago was found dismembered in a black garbage bag."

Sarah walked back to her chair. "Why her and not the others?"

"We don't know, but we guess she died earlier than the other one found with her in the cage."

"How can you tell that after twelve years?"

"Human remains tell us a grand story. All you have to do is know how to read the signs and know where to look."

"Can you explain?"

Maria cleared her throat. "Sealed containers holding dead bodies are taken to the police department's lab where they are fumigated for prints. You'd probably guess that we're looking for a professional, so no prints were found. The remains go to the medical examiner where a postmortem begins."

"And …"

Lyson and Justin sat quietly, listening. Sarah found a new respect for Lyson—a cop near retirement but intent on solving one last case. So intent he was willing to explore drastic measures, like contacting Sarah.

"A forensic anthropologist is brought in to handle bodies found after this period of time. We start with a timeline based on the victimology report. This will give us an estimated time of death, but forensic anthropology doesn't work too fast. Luckily, that letter Lyson got was actually from the Unsub directing us to the bodies. Therefore, we've already got a workable timeline of two bodies every four years."

"You said Unsub. Remind me what that is."

"Unidentified subject. The killer. Something to note—sometimes they like to follow their own cases."

Sarah nodded. "You mean through the newspapers?"

"Yes, and in other ways. Sometimes they'll call into Crime Stoppers."

"What for?" Sarah asked.

"Every time the Crime Stoppers Hotline is called, a report is generated, and for every call, there's a follow-up by an officer in this task force. We follow every lead. You can never be too sure."

"Wow," Sarah said, scanning their faces. "That's a lot of man-hours." She brought her attention back to Maria. "Tell me more. How did you learn about the crisis center connection? What if the Unsub knew his victims? Isn't that common in murder cases? I mean, maybe he worked there."

"You're right. It's common. But not in this case. If murder is personal, the murderer is driven to attack the victim's face, hands, or hair. Sometimes the murderer feels shame and regrets what they have done, so they cover the face of the victim as if the victim could see them for who they really are even though the victim is already dead."

"That didn't happen in this case?"

Maria shook her head. "No, this was clinical. Like a

doctor. Each woman had her tongue removed and cauterized. He didn't want them to bleed out."

Sarah leaned back. "That's horrible."

"The worst part was how they died."

"I'm afraid to ask."

"We have gathered that the murderer doesn't feed them or give them any water to drink. Nothing at all. Their stomachs were virtually empty. But he abuses them for the week or so he has them until they die from the cold and thirst. He leaves them naked, exposed to the elements, starving, and weakened. After a week or ten days, he locks the cage and walks away on what we've since learned is February 29 every four years. A psychological profile is being prepared, but it does appear that he has a certain kind of hatred toward women and the things they say, hence the ritualistic removal of the tongue."

"Methodical. Clinical. Insane."

"Exactly," Lyson piped in. "That's why we must stop him this time, or he'll disappear for four years. Since we only have five days until he leaves his next victims, he probably already has them, their tongues removed."

Sarah shuddered.

"Is there anything about this from Vivian?" Lyson asked. "Does any of this coincide with what she has been telling you?"

Sarah thought about it, going over the messages in her head, but nothing seemed remotely close except for the crisis center.

"The only thing is the …"

"Crisis center," Justin finished for her.

She turned back to Maria. "Tell me about the one found

in the garbage bag. Why was she different?"

"We're speculating that she died early."

"How so? Why?"

"At this late stage, we have nothing to base it on. The first two were found in a field, buried in a huge hole, which was so big that a man could climb down inside and walk around bent over slightly. Something like a bunker from the war. We found powdered chlorine as fine and white as sugar. It's meant to keep the coyotes away from dead bodies. He wanted us to discover these women and the state he had left them."

"This guy sounds like a piece of work."

Lyson picked his pen up and tapped it on the table. "That's why we need him off the streets. Is there anything you can do to help?"

Sarah took a moment to examine everything. Was Vivian pointing her in the direction of working with the police? Was the purpose of going to the crisis center only to meet Lyson and have him recognize her? If so, why not where he buys his coffee or his donuts? Why the crisis center? Or could the girl she saved be the purpose?

"I can tell you that I was at the crisis center for a reason. Sure, you saw me there." She gestured at Lyson. "But there has to be something else."

"We're already looking into it," Justin said. "Since we discovered that particular crisis center was visited by at least five of the six women before they were reported missing, we've been looking at employees and ex-employees all the way back to twelve years ago. So far, nothing has come up, but we're still looking. People change jobs; volunteers move around. We have nothing solid yet. The only employee that's been there that long has a tight track record. Never been involved with the law."

"Are you referring to Jennifer?" Sarah asked. "She talked to me. Could she be of interest?"

"I've known Jennifer for half a dozen years," Lyson piped in. "She's clean. We checked her out first, just in case."

"Something has me stuck on her," Sarah said. "Have you looked into her family, maybe a boyfriend? Who does she pillow talk to? That's where I'd start."

"We did start there, but we're going deeper. Just in case."

Justin was jotting notes.

"Can you tell us what Vivian has got planned for you?" Lyson asked. "The fact that you were told to go to the crisis center and lie leads me to believe that you're drawing the Unsub out somehow."

"If I am, he will never make it to trial. A man like that only deserves a violent end and then an unmarked grave." No one said a word, so she continued. "I need assurances."

"What kind of assurances?" Lyson asked.

"If I tell you what I'm supposed to do, you stay out of it. It has to go down, as Vivian says, or people die. It's always been that way."

Justin leaned over and whispered something in Lyson's ear.

Sarah almost called him out for it but exercised restraint.

We're either being honest and open, or we're not.

But they had been forthcoming. She didn't want to hurt the rapport they had built.

"It depends on what you tell us," Lyson said. "We're bound to investigate leads. We have to take the lead if you know something that could help us. So I can't give you any assurances."

"Then I have no idea how I can help. I guess we're done here."

"That's the wrong answer," Lyson said. "I'm retiring in just over a month. I won't let this asshole go for another four years. If you know something, you have to tell us." He pushed his chair out and stood. "Or I'll have to arrest you for obstruction of justice."

"See what I mean? How can I trust you when this is how you treat me?" Sarah stood too. "Relax. I'm sure none of what Vivian has asked me to do is related."

"Then let us in it."

"Since it's not related, I won't."

"How can you be so sure it's not related?"

What if he had a point? If there was something to it, she had to at least try. This guy couldn't be allowed to spend the next four years a free man.

Before she convinced herself not to speak, she said, "In about four hours, I need to be somewhere."

"We're listening."

"At this place, I am going to stop a man from meeting with a thirteen-year-old girl who has been lying about her age online. They're supposed to meet to travel the world together. He has been luring her for some time now. He's in his fifties. All I know is where to be and when. Then it's done."

"And you feel confident this man is not our guy?"

"Absolutely. The little girl has never been to the crisis center. Not at her age."

"Okay," Lyson said. "I don't think any of that matters anymore."

"Good," Sarah said. "I need to leave so I can change out

of this stupid top—"

"No, Sarah. It doesn't matter anymore because you are under arrest for aiding and abetting a murderer. I'm not playing games anymore."

"What? That's ridiculous. You're bluffing."

"Afraid not. Unless you give us the details of where this meeting is to take place and everything else Vivian has told you. Sounds like you have four hours to decide where you want to spend the night. In jail or at home."

The door to the conference room burst open, smacking into the wall. The two FBI agents from last night bustled in, followed by three Toronto officers in uniform.

"What is this?" Lyson shouted. "Why are you two here?"

"One more word out of you, Dinosaur, and your retirement starts tonight." The FBI agent turned to Sarah. "Get up. We're leaving."

"She's not going anywhere." Lyson moved between them. "You're in a Toronto police station on Canadian soil. Since when does the FBI operate up here with impunity?"

"Since your boss sanctioned it." No one moved. "We warned you off Sarah last night. Now you arrest her to get her down here?"

"I didn't just arrest her, you imbecile." Lyson sounded pissed now. "She shot a man. Then approached my officers with a weapon instead of being unarmed. She stays here with us."

Sarah tried to remember the FBI agent's name as he stepped up and stood less than a foot from Lyson.

"Sarah is coming with us, and you and your army of monkeys will stay away from her for the remaining time she is in your city, or I won't just take your job. I'll ruin your life.

Forget you even know this girl is alive." The agent moved closer. Sarah thought he was going to touch Lyson's nose. "Are we clear?"

The other agent stood tense, his hands far to the side, watching the Toronto cops for a reaction. Sarah tensed, the air thick.

"Get out of my face," Lyson whispered. "Sarah, you know what we're up against. Help us if you can. We need you."

She walked around to face Lyson. "That's it? You give up? You're going to release me into their custody?"

"I've got nothing on you, and they know it."

"So what was all that bullshit about the night in jail? Now you can see why I don't trust cops." She swung around and faced the FBI men. "That goes for you, too. Whatever it is you've got planned won't work. The Sophia Project men tried. They're all dead. I'm still free. So I'd be careful how close you get to me."

"Is that a threat?"

Sarah walked past them and left the room. "No, it's the truth. They are all dead."

Chapter 20

HE HAD FINISHED WITH both of their tongues and made sure the bleeding had stopped, using the chloroform as often as needed to keep them asleep. The sun was rising, heralding his exit. The tracks dragged in the snow needed to be kicked out. Getting his vehicle out of the area was important to reduce its visibility until he came back again in the evening. Two more days of work, and then he could stay with his mannequins until the end.

He would deliver the second letter with Alan Lyson's name on it soon.

Then the game would come to an end, a day he looked forward to.

On his way upstairs and out of the warehouse, he shut as many doors as possible to keep the noise down if his dolls were to wake up and start pounding on the metal or moaning too loud.

He opened the side door and peeked outside. The morning was crisp and clear, the air cold. Not a single cloud littered the blue sky. Traffic in the distance had picked up, but not too many people were in this area yet, as it was just before seven. The sun hadn't crested the horizon yet.

He hopped out the door and walked backward, kicking at the snow as he did, his balls still aching from the squeeze Melanie had put on them. She was the only one who had a small ID packet with her cash in it under the rim of her panties. His original subject didn't, but he already knew her name.

Today's lunch was on Melanie. She'd had over five hundred dollars in her little purse.

His backside bumped the fence by the hole. After squeezing through backward, he turned to walk to his Range Rover. He reflected on how lucky both of his subjects were. He had spent four years waiting for last night. His first night with another subject. And all he accomplished was the tongue removal. He didn't get any pleasure from their bodies other than admiring them from afar. His member was too sore. If only Melanie hadn't been there last night, everything would've worked out for the better.

But tonight would be different. After he had used them up and made them bleed, he would make Melanie pay for her interference in ways she had never dreamed of.

The price of his sore balls was little for the pleasure he would get making his mannequins pay a much steeper price.

The ultimate reset fixed their wrongs.

In the end, he was doing them a favor, even if they didn't realize it.

The truth was, he was doing the world a favor.

Chapter 21

SARAH LED THE WAY through the maze of halls and rooms on the second floor of the police station, heading for the exit. The FBI men trailed her like they had been doing for months.

At the door, before walking out into the cold, she turned to them. "What is it you want? Who in the FBI would task you two to stay on me? Are you protecting me, watching my back, or hunting me for some reason?"

"Not here," one of them said. "Across the street. The coffee shop. We'll talk there."

"Okay, but I leave within the hour. I have somewhere to go."

"Fine. One hour. We'll drive you where you have to go."

They stepped outside, and the one who did all the talking took his suit jacket off and wrapped it around Sarah's shoulders. Her jacket was left at the massage parlor, ruined after being used as a tourniquet.

"Shit. My gun. I forgot to pick up my gun. They were going to give it back to me when I left."

"We talk first. Then we'll come back and get it for you. I promise."

She thought about it for a moment. She couldn't use it at the Toronto airport where she was supposed to help the thirteen-year-old, so she agreed. Lyson probably wouldn't release it to anyone but her anyway.

They took a table in the rear corner of the coffee shop. Sarah sat with her back to the wall so she could see the door and everything else in the small shop. The one who did the talking walked over to the counter and ordered for the three of them.

The other one sat across from her.

"Do you talk?" she asked.

He nodded.

"Sounds like it."

"I talk. But Special Agent Kierian runs this operation."

"Oh, this is an operation now?"

"He'll tell you all about it."

"I can't wait." She clapped her hands together and rubbed them in mock anticipation.

Kierian joined them with fresh coffee and muffins. Sarah grabbed the whole wheat one and devoured it, washing it down with the coffee, not realizing just how hungry she had been. Nor how much coffee she'd been drinking today.

"I said an hour," she started. "You are down to forty-five minutes. If you've got something to say, talk fast."

"Why are those cops harassing you?"

"I could ask you the same thing. What's with shadowing me?"

"I'm Special Agent Penn Kierian. This is Special Agent Tower Clint. Nice to meet you, Sarah Roberts."

She nodded.

"It is Sarah Roberts, right?" Kierian asked.

Sarah gripped her coffee cup and looked at Clint. "Is Kierian for real? You have to ask me that after five months. By now, I'd expect you to know the kind of toothpaste I use."

Clint stayed silent.

Kierian said, "I mean, *the* Sarah Roberts."

"Why are you saying it like that?" she asked.

"Because it doesn't impress me much."

She let go of her cup and leaned back in her chair, her leg tapping to the soft music from the speakers above.

"I'm not trying to impress anybody."

"Then how come the Toronto cops are interested in you?"

"I shot a guy before lunch."

Kierian whistled through his teeth. "You shot a guy before lunch? What's happening before dinner?"

"Stay tuned. Don't change the station."

"You're not going to tell me why Alan Lyson has such an interest in you, are you?"

"I just did."

"Is it the Leap Year Killer?"

Sarah didn't flinch. "You're down to thirty-five minutes of that hour. Please don't tell me you're here to talk about Lyson and the Toronto Police Department. If you want to know what they want with me, ask them."

Kierian and Clint both sipped from their coffees at the same time. Kierian set his down and wrapped an arm over the backrest of his chair.

He was getting ready for the serious part of the conversation. There was something about him that she liked. He had discipline. Anyone could tell that by looking at his flat stomach and lean face. When he smiled, she could almost see the dozen-plus muscles in his face, each moving to form that smile. He never frowned, and wrinkles hadn't set in yet. He didn't smoke, and age hadn't bothered with him either.

"You're in the papers from time to time," Kierian said. "The media loves you."

"That's their problem. I don't ask for that shit. I'd prefer they leave me out of it."

"Everyone whispers your name. It sounds like they're talking about a Hollywood star, a celebrity."

"I didn't ask for that, either. I stayed off the radar for as long as possible when I started out."

"But now you're all grown up." He took the first bite of his muffin and chased it with coffee. After he swallowed, he said, "Tell me something. Do you believe in the other side?"

"Are you for real? You use considerable influence to yank me from police custody to discuss spirituality?"

"No. It's just I don't believe in it. At least not in how you claim to operate."

"Good. Next question. Next." She stopped tapping her leg. She wasn't nervous, just getting angry now.

"That doesn't bother you?"

"What you believe is none of my concern. It doesn't matter if you believe in God or not because He believes in you. We're all His children, and we all go home in the end. That's it. But I think God has stopped keeping score. We're born, we die. Just not in the way you think. It's the other way around."

"How so?"

"The real death is coming here."

He raised his eyebrows and glanced at Clint to ensure he was listening.

Sarah continued. "We leave our home," she pointed upward, "and come here. When we're done down here in the swamp of humanity, whatever you want to call it, we go home to our real home. We all do. No choice. Whether you believe it or not. That's why I have no problem sending a bad guy on his way. Just trying to make a life for the rest of us stuck here for the next few decades easier."

"Is that what you would tell an atheist like me?"

"How come I feel you're wasting my time?"

"I'm leading up to something."

"Stop leading. Just get there."

"Impatient?"

"No. You're trying my patience. I don't play games, and I don't bluff. I say it how it is. Life is easier that way. If someone doesn't like what I have to say, then that's something they have to deal with. It isn't my problem. Be more confident in who you are and what you believe."

"Okay, then I'll just say it. I don't believe in you."

"No one asked you to."

"No, I'm serious. I believe you had a sister that you lost, but there's no way she sends you messages from the other side. Impossible. It's all a lie."

Sarah's smile widened. This whole time, the other agent remained quiet. He turned to watch the door and glanced at some of the other patrons as if he wasn't listening, but he was.

"What is your point?" Sarah asked. "Trying to stir self-doubt in me?"

"All I'm saying is, Vivian isn't real."

"Then tell me, bright boy, where do the prophecies come from?"

"You, and only you. Just like Esmerelda Hall. You remember her? The psychic woman from the psychic fair all those years ago? What about Dolan Ryan? These are people like you who are actually able to feel or see something. But the future psychic stuff, that's you. That's your forte. You get detailed analyses of crimes and accidents, which makes your gift even better. Sounds to me like a hidden desire to be a cop. Maybe that's why you hate them so much. Are you jealous you can't be one?"

Some of what he was saying filtered in. She wondered if it could be true. Could she be the psychic one, using Vivian as the crutch?

"Look at it like this," she said. "You've got two options whether you believe in God or not. Say you don't believe, and there really is life after death. Then you're fucked. But let's say you believe. If you're wrong and there's nothing but dirt on your corpse, you're just as fucked. The only other option is to believe in God; if you're right, paradise awaits you. That's the organized religion analysis. As far as I'm concerned, we all go home whether we believe or not because a God of love would never offer ultimatums about believing in him or burning in a lake of fire. That's all bullshit. There is no Lucifer, no devil. He's manmade to scare children into doing the right thing before the times of a civil society." Sweat trickled down her back. Heat rose to her face as she spoke, her words laced with emotion and belief. "The only devil is the beast inside us all that hurts others.

Madmen, murderers, rapists, those are Lucifers. That's why I love hurting or killing them. I'm doing the world a favor. Next time, don't judge me. Next time just say thank you and walk away. Now, are we done here?"

"Okay, nice speech. If we had more time, I'm sure you could sell me on that. But I still don't believe in Vivian."

"Then don't. Means little to me." Sarah looked past Kierian's shoulder as two rough-looking men entered the coffee shop and stopped at the door, searching the tables. Their eyes landed on her. They glared for a prolonged second, then looked away and walked to the counter.

"You okay?" Kierian asked.

"Those two guys who just walked in seemed interested in us."

Kierian and Clint looked at the same time.

"They look like AOV," Kierian said.

"AOV? What's that?"

Kierian turned back to her. "Angels of Violence."

"How can you tell from just looking at them?" Sarah asked.

"Because of those tattoos. AOV is famous for covering their bodies with tattoos, especially their faces. They almost always have the AOV across their forehead, cheeks, or just under their chin on the neck. Somewhere visible so on the street they're easily recognizable."

"That sounds stupid. Aren't there anti-gang laws now? Openly labeling yourself as one would bring the authorities down on you fast."

"That's the problem with AOV. They're not called the Angels of Violence for nothing. There are over seventy different street gangs on the streets of Toronto alone, but these guys stand out because they revel in violence, live by it, and initiate themselves into the gang with it. Their respect for authority is void. Police who arrest them are targeted. Lawyers who fail them, judges who judge them. It doesn't matter how high-ranking the authority is in the justice system. No one is safe from these guys. To them, we're all the enemy."

"Wow, how do you two know so much about Toronto's gang population if you're FBI from the States?"

"Watching you for five months has been boring. We've had time on our hands to read about the city we're stationed in, from the local papers to researching the criminal element."

"Fair enough. It sounds like the Angels of Violence need to be taken off the streets completely."

"We wish. In 2005, the FBI helped create the National Gang Intelligence Center so we could all better understand them, catalog them, and make arrests that stick, keeping as many off the streets for as long as we could."

The AOV men bought coffees and turned to find a table near the door. Only once did the taller one look back at her again.

"Why are they paying attention to us then?" Sarah asked. "They know you two?"

"We don't know them, but they can probably tell we're cops or something like it. We're right across the street from the Toronto Police building. Actually, that's probably why they're here. Visiting a member in jail or something. Anyway, back to our discussion." Kierian downed the last of his coffee. "I was saying that Vivian isn't real. Would you agree with that?"

"Absolutely not. Vivian told me her name before I even knew I had a sister. My parents sheltered me from her death when I was young. When I asked them about her, they came clean."

"I think it's because you're psychic that you could pull from wherever it is you get your information. Is it possible that your psyche attached itself to her, using her as the message giver so you would be better able to handle what was happening to you at a time in your life when you were coming out of a depression? I understand you were once a puller?"

Sarah leaned forward, violated by this conversation. "How the hell do you know so much about me?"

"Official interviews by law enforcement officers going back to when you first saved Mary Bennett. I've read everything in every file all the way up to and including Vegas. Quite impressive. Don't get me wrong. I admire you. But I want to meet the real Sarah, not the one who doesn't know who she is."

He had raised enough questions that she needed time to go over it. She asked for another coffee. Kierian got up to order her one. His partner didn't say a word while he was gone.

Both AOV members watched Kierian the whole time. Sarah was starting to get the feeling they were here for them or her, not visiting a member in jail across the street.

Her thoughts were drawn back to the questions Kierian had raised. What if it were true? Would the messages change? If she was the psychic one and there really wasn't a dead sister involved, could she evolve and do more? Instead of just stopping criminals or putting herself in danger, could she help people in their time of need? Mothers who had lost children. Children who had lost parents. Could she talk to the dead and ease the pain of the living?

Why did Vivian go silent for the last five months? It wasn't like crimes weren't happening in and around Toronto. It would make sense if it were just Sarah all this time. The five-month hiatus was so she could explore her relationship with Aaron. Was it self-imposed? Or was Vivian protecting her from these men?

She wondered what was on Kierian's agenda. He was still leading her somewhere. Maybe he was trying to get her to admit something. Her suspicion of his motives grew.

Maybe I should have a lawyer present.

He returned to the table and placed a steaming coffee in front of her. She sipped it twice and then recoiled.

Too much coffee today.

"Are you friend or foe?" she asked.

"Friend."

"And how am I supposed to know that? Just because you tell me?"

"You're psychic. Figure it out."

She looked between the two of them. "Are we done here?"

"No. I have a couple more questions."

"I need to make a call first," Sarah said. "Lend me your cell phone."

Kierian reached into his breast pocket and produced one. "You're not going to take off, are you?"

"Of course not. You're my ride. I need to be at the Toronto Airport in an hour."

"Good. We'll take you."

She grabbed the phone and stepped away. "I'll be in the ladies' room. Back in a sec."

Kierian nodded. Clint's attention was on the AOV men, who seemed intent on staring back at them.

In the bathroom, she called Aaron. He picked up immediately.

"Aaron …"

"Sarah! Where are you? No one is telling me anything."

"I'm fine. The massage parlor had a little problem, but I expected that. Why else would Vivian send me there?"

"A little problem. The news channels say an unknown assailant shot a gang member in the leg. The police aren't releasing names."

"A gang member?" Her mind raced. "Did they say the gang's name?"

"Something violence. Or Hell's Angels."

"Could it have been the Angels of Violence?"

"Yeah, that's it. Why?"

"No reason." She leaned into the wall by the hand dryer and stared at herself in the mirror, her stomach acid mixing at the thought the AOV men in the coffee shop were there for her.

"Sarah, I've got news for you."

"What?"

"Your voice … are you okay?"

"Yeah, go ahead. Tell me."

"Russell called."

That perked her up. "My cousin?"

"Yes."

"What did he say?"

Aaron told her what Russell said about the fire and bomb

and how she would die if she didn't stop now.

"If I stopped every time I was warned, I should never have started in the first place."

"But Sarah, you told me about Vegas and how Russell was instrumental in saving your life. Sounds to me like he's trying to do that again."

"Fire? Bombs? Well then, I guess I'm fucked because I have no other choice."

"Sarah, you do have a choice …"

"No," she shouted in the small room, her voice echoing off the walls. "I will not let a man take a thirteen-year-old girl from the airport to rape her. If I can stop him, I will not let the Leap Year Killer continue his killing spree. Not while I'm alive and kicking. I'll do my best to not work with the police because they all seem to be serious assholes, but I'll continue doing what Vivian tells me to do."

A moment of doubt wondered if it was Vivian after all.

"Sarah, seriously—"

"Aaron, I'll be home tonight. We'll talk then." She hit end and tightened her fist around the phone. "Shit."

The messages had been specific. Visit the crisis center, lie about the abuse, and then blame herself for it. Apply for a job at that massage parlor.

Then the message from a few days ago supplied her with an address on Keele Street North. And a time she had to be there. Vivian had called it the end game. But the instructions were to keep the building clear. That meant the police, too. Don't visit early. Nothing. Go there at the time in the message but do not enter the building.

At least, that's how she interpreted what Vivian had written through Sarah's pen.

When she walked out to the table, Kierian had finished his coffee. They appeared ready to go.

"Everything good?" he asked.

She nodded and handed Kierian's phone back.

"You look pissed off."

"I am. Vivian and I had a chat," she lied. Whether he believed in her sister or not, she would give Vivian the credit on this one.

"And?" Kierian asked.

"When we're done at the airport, I need you to introduce yourself to a bomb-sniffing dog. Meet his handler. Then use your power as a high-ranking FBI guy and commandeer his services for the later part of this week."

"And why would I do that?"

"For my cooperation. I will work with you under certain conditions if you work with me. Deal?"

"Deal. What conditions? And why a bomb-sniffing dog?"

"So I don't get killed at the end of this. It's shaping up to be a horrible week, and I was just told that I die at the end, and there's nothing I can do about it. Great, huh?"

Chapter 22

COLIN JAMES TOOK OFF late for his lunch. He had wanted to stay in his office long enough to see if the Canadian Protection Services Range Rover returned to the warehouse across the street.

When he arrived for work this morning and glanced across the street, he had seen fresh tracks in the snow that cut a path to the hole in the fence. But he had responsibilities and a job to do, and playing neighborhood security man would only see him without a job and standing on the unemployment line. Bruce had seemed nice enough, looked educated, and drove a Range Rover.

What could be the trouble?

Only that he was in an abandoned building, and CPS was a defunct company. When he looked them up, he discovered Canadian Protection Services was the old name for a new company formed many years ago called Group 4. When he called them, he learned that no one was charged to patrol the building across the street. He had been tempted to call the police at that time. Even had the phone in his hand, suspended in the air, but he had replaced the phone, intent on asking Bruce himself. Maybe there was something else going on, and Colin James wasn't so much of a Nosy Parker that he could spoil it for Bruce.

But those new tracks in the snow bothered him. And now that it was mid-afternoon and the Range Rover hadn't made an appearance, maybe it was time for a reconnaissance mission.

With the Range Rover not there, this might be his best chance to see what Bruce was up to.

Colin pushed away from his desk, removed his headset, and walked down the row of cubicles to the water cooler. He had to remove three jackets to get to his on the coat rack.

He stuck his head in his boss's office. "Barb?"

She stopped writing and looked up from the mess of papers on her desk.

"Taking a fifteen-minute break. That okay?"

She nodded and went back to her work.

Colin slipped on his winter boots and stepped outside. The cold air hit him hard after spending the last five-plus hours in the warm office.

He took a deep breath and started down the salted path toward the company parking lot. Once across the street, he checked both ways and waited for a moment in case Bruce showed up.

The road remained empty.

From this close, the path in the snow looked messed up on purpose. The snow on either side was almost two feet high and untouched. But in the center of the path, it was packed down with the sides brushed back and forth as if someone did it with their boot.

He didn't like that. Every suspicious bone in his body called out. Something was wrong here. Very wrong.

He started along beside the path, lifting his feet high to break new snow. If Bruce was up to something illegal, he didn't want to mar the evidence for the authorities.

He easily squeezed through the hole in the fence and continued to the side door of the old warehouse. He opened the door cautiously, almost expecting something to be waiting for him.

"Too many horror movies," he whispered to himself.

Once inside, he undid his jacket and scanned the area. Nothing seemed to have been moved or changed.

Maybe it's on the lower floor where Bruce came from the other day.

He started for the stairs that led to the floor below, his stomach a ball of knots in anticipation of what he would find.

Something clanged inside the building somewhere, and he stopped so suddenly that he almost lost his balance. Hairs rose on the back of his neck.

What the hell was that?

The metallic clanging came again.

He wasn't so sure he wanted to see what was down there. The Range Rover driver might have a pet alligator he's keeping alive or an ape of some kind, two living creatures Colin James never wanted to see live. Alligators were too fast, and their mouths were half the size of their bodies, and with all those teeth—apes were strong and fast and could dangle from anything, and their screech was enough to chill his bones and—

The clanging came again. This time it happened twice. It wasn't Morse code. Too slow. It was almost as if someone was doing it out of boredom.

Maybe that's all it is. Boredom.

He put one foot in front of the other and started down the stairs. The floor below didn't get as much sun, but there was enough light to navigate. He walked across the length of the floor, listening to the clanging the whole way.

The clanging came from behind the closed door to the back room. It drew him like a beacon, a lighthouse on a stormy sea, hypnotized by the sound.

He stood beside the door, listening.

Someone moaned. He was sure of it. Maybe they were meeting inside, and he would be in trouble for trespassing. Why did he think he could just walk into this abandoned warehouse when a security guard named Bruce told him to stay out?

The clanging again, like a rock on a piece of metal.

Why would someone do that in a meeting?

Something loud banged upstairs. He almost jumped out of his winter boots.

Someone was running across the floor above him, no doubt headed for the stairs that led to where he stood in the open by the last door on the basement level.

He pulled out his cell phone and dialed 911.

The reception was low down here, but a woman came on the line and asked if he needed police, fire, or ambulance.

"Police."

There was a click, and a man answered.

The person above was on the stairs now. The clanging

inside the room intensified.

Colin James opened the door with his right hand and walked inside.

"Officer, I'm on Keele Street north at—" he stopped when he saw the cage. Two women were inside it, naked, on the cold floor. The open door cast light on their faces. What looked like dried blood had crusted on and around their open mouths. They were huddled in the corner of the cage, and one of them had her arm out, tapping the bar beside her head.

"Sir, what is the emergency?" the officer asked on his cell phone.

But Colin couldn't find his voice. The horror in front of him had shocked him into paralysis. Footsteps bounded up behind him.

In that second, he knew he was a dead man if he didn't speak soon. Bruce was bad. Bruce had women as pets, locked away in a cage. Who knew what horror he had preyed upon them?

And the blood.

But now Bruce was running up behind him and would kill him for seeing his secret. Colin had watched enough movies to know how it all worked.

He never did find his voice. The officer yelled in his ear but then clicked off, most likely thinking the call was a prank.

Then Colin James lost consciousness.

The last thing he heard before going under was the clanging of metal, loud, fast, and sharp.

Chapter 23

SARAH WALKED BEHIND KIERIAN with Clint behind her as they left the coffee shop. The AOV members watched them leave, a stupid grin on their faces. Both of them looked like accomplished street fighters with energy bouncing off their skin. As Kierian hit the door, the gang members got up to follow.

Once outside, Kierian grabbed Sarah and pulled her back to the wall. Both FBI men shielded her until the two AOV men emerged from the shop.

Kierian put his hand on the butt of his weapon. "I'm Special Agent Kierian with the FBI. Why are you following us?"

Both members only had eyes for Sarah. They stared at her past Kierian's shoulder.

"I asked you a question."

The alpha of the two looked at Kierian slowly. He

twisted his neck sideways and cracked it. He smiled, with at least three missing teeth. He had either spent some serious time in jail or fought bare-knuckle matches for fun.

"Not following you, ese. Just admiring that pretty thing you got."

"Then move along. Nothing to see here."

No one moved for a moment. The alpha raised his arm and pointed at Sarah. "We'll see you later when your dogs are sleeping. We have a debt to settle."

They backed away for twenty feet, then turned and walked with a mock limp until they disappeared around the corner.

"What the hell was that all about?" Kierian asked.

"Probably about that guy I shot this morning."

Kierian faced her. "You don't want to owe a debt to AOV. When they collect, you're either in the hospital for a few weeks, paralyzed for life, or in the morgue."

"I'll be fine. Just get me to the airport."

Sarah still had Kierian's jacket wrapped around her shoulders as they walked down the sidewalk to the Impala. Traffic was light, and getting out of downtown proved easy.

Once on the Gardiner Expressway, they made good time to the 427 and onto the airport exit.

"Tell us more about what you've got to do here," Kierian said.

"All I know is a man has been luring a thirteen-year-old girl. He's on a 5:25 p.m. flight from Detroit. The girl ran away from her school this morning and took the bus to get here, per the instructions this man gave her. No one knows she's going to be here. Her parents will only start to be worried by the time their daughter will be meeting this pig."

"Anything else?"

"If I don't stop the meeting, that girl will never come home."

"And you got all this in a note from Vivian?"

"No, I found it in a box of Cracker Jacks."

Kierian met her eyes in the rearview and then looked away. He parked in the drop-off part of departures and showed his ID to a cop on duty.

The cop nodded and continued to wave traffic through.

The trio got out and walked through the sliding doors.

"It's close to five," Clint said. "We still have time."

"Good. Then buy me something."

Kierian smiled. "What does little Sarah Roberts want?"

"Don't ever call me little. I'm smaller than you, but that kind of thing pisses me off."

"Fair enough. No little."

"Now you owe me."

"I owe you?"

"Yeah. I could've gone home to change. I had time after my talk with Lyson. But now I'm stuck in this stupid top with my items hanging out. I need a new shirt or a sweater. You're buying."

"Who says?"

"I do." She walked away and headed toward the shopping area. "Don't they give you a budget? Someone sent you here to get something out of me and paid a lot of money for months of surveillance. Buying a fucking shirt is the least you could do for a girl."

Kierian and Clint exchanged a smile, then followed Sarah. After fifteen minutes, she had a T-shirt that said *I Love Toronto* on it and a thick sweater to wear over that.

Kierian led the way to the monitors that detailed the flight arrival times. The flight from Detroit was right on time. They went to the gates where everyone from that plane would enter the common area of the airport.

Kierian pulled a member of airport security aside and explained that they were waiting for a man to deplane from the Detroit flight. He said they had credible evidence that this man was here to kidnap a youth that he had lured to the airport.

While he arranged backup from airport security and explained how important it was to stay out of sight, Sarah backed away and watched the waiting crowd, searching for a young girl standing alone.

While they waited, she thought about the Angels of Violence and what they said about a debt. If they were after her, how come Vivian hadn't said anything? Unless this was why she went to the massage parlor, to roust them. Sometimes it was maddening not knowing what Vivian's intentions were. Most times, her blind faith got her through, but things seemed more dangerous, more severe this time. She hated being unarmed and unprepared.

Aaron was a capable fighter who could maim five men in a fight. What would Aaron think if she had told him that she had brought these FBI men with her instead of him? He would be hurt. But everything happens for a reason. Sarah had learned to go with the flow and let it happen. There was something about how things worked out: Sarah always knew Vivian had read the playbook weeks before and only told Sarah what she needed to hear and when to keep her on point.

When this was done, and Sarah was back at the

apartment later that night, she figured she and Aaron would have to have *the* talk. Could their budding relationship last with who she was? Would he understand her enough to let her go so she could learn to love him? Trying to control her would never work. She would rather be single forever than have a man run things for her. Why couldn't men just be happy to be in a relationship, share things, go to movies, have dinner, and have sex? Yes, wild sex. Why wasn't that enough? Women weren't property, most of all a woman like Sarah.

She resolved to make that clear to Aaron later.

The double doors opened, and people piled into the airport, pulling luggage behind them. The clock by the arrivals monitor said it was fifteen minutes to six. The Detroit flight had deplaned, and people had time to grab their luggage.

At any second, the fateful meeting would take place.

Kierian caught her eye. He shrugged. She looked away and studied the crowd even harder, but the only children she saw were with their mother or another adult.

A girl about the age they were looking for stood off the side behind a pillar. She looked shy and confused. A second later, a woman walked over and scolded her for standing too far away. She took her hand and guided her back to a stroller where an infant waited.

"We wait for Daddy together," the mother said, loud enough for everyone to hear.

Sarah looked at Clint. His attention was on the people entering the airport. Kierian was talking to a security guard again twenty feet back.

Normal activity everywhere. Yet, in minutes a meeting

was about to take place. A meeting they had to stop.

Sarah decided to do what Clint was doing. Process of elimination. She would study the people entering the airport. All men with someone would be written off as not a potential. For every man that appeared to be alone, she would try to follow his movements for as long as she could without leaving the area.

After another dozen people, a single man came into view. In his forties at least, a backpack slung over his shoulder and walking steadily. His hair was greased back, and he looked slimy enough to prey on the young and weak. This had to be the guy. He pulled a cell phone from his pocket and typed furiously, no doubt texting someone that he had arrived.

She looked away, watched for others, and then double-checked that the man was gone and not meeting someone. He walked through the sliding doors heading outside toward a taxi, his arm in the air hailing one.

Another man emerged. This one caught Clint's attention, so Sarah focused back on the people still filing through. A good-looking, tall man walked out and searched the crowd until his eyes stopped on a woman in her twenties. They called out to each other, and she ran at him, jumping into his arms. Sarah longed for Aaron.

More single men exited the doors. Men in suits, men with cell phones, men with oversized luggage. One pulled something big enough to carry golf clubs. Another had a guitar over his shoulder.

The steady flow of traffic finally decreased. The door opened randomly, and an odd person came through.

Kierian headed toward her.

If this didn't come together, it would mean two things.

One, a thirteen-year-old girl would be in serious trouble somewhere, and two, the FBI would think her psychic abilities were a hoax.

She couldn't care less what anyone thought. The girl was the priority.

"Now what?" Kierian asked.

"He was here. He had to be. Vivian is never wrong."

"We watched everyone. No single man met a young girl from that plane. Unless he still has to come out, I don't see any young girls waiting around here, and it's almost six."

"I know. Let me think."

She did a full turn, looking around the area. She stopped at the window to the outside. The sun had dropped. Smoke billowed from idling cars.

Something wasn't right. Maybe the perp instructed the girl to meet him somewhere else. That had to be it. They were standing at the wrong spot.

Of course. He wouldn't meet her in a crowd.

She walked toward the window.

"Sarah?" Kierian said, but she ignored him.

At the window, she looked both ways, up and down the arrival's temporary parking.

The man with the backpack slung over his shoulder, and the greasy hair from earlier was knelt by a taxi cab's open door.

Her eyes widened.

He was talking to a young girl with pretty red hair. The young girl appeared anxious and was shaking her head. From where Sarah was, it seemed the girl was crying.

"Fuck!"

Everything inside Sarah screamed. She had found the

perp.

"Got him," she said to Kierian and started to run.

"Where?" he yelled after her.

"Tell airport security he's about to get into a cab."

She dodged a slow-moving couple, landed on the carpet, and weaved to the right around a man pushing a cart overloaded with luggage, and then had to slow to let the automatic doors open in time.

"Hurry, dammit!" she yelled at the doors.

Then through another set of doors, moving just as slow.

Once through them, she turned to the right.

The man and the little girl were gone.

The taxi was already a hundred yards away, slowing for a speed bump.

"Sarah?" Kierian said from behind her.

"In that cab up ahead. The one slowing for a speed bump. Have somebody stop it."

She ran. As fast as her legs could pump, she ran. Inside, she screamed for that little girl who was about to leave and be gone for good. She looked back once and saw Kierian coming behind her on his cell phone.

The cab was getting away.

She ran harder, knowing she could never catch up with it.

The airport exit was just ahead of the cab. The speed bumps were the only saving grace. People with luggage in a crosswalk stopped the cab, allowing Sarah time to make some ground, but she was already getting winded, and the brake lights of the cab turned off as it moved forward again.

Once it turned the corner, it would be lost from sight.

There was nothing left to do, and Kierian's car was too far away to give chase.

Unless she stole a car or jumped in a cab herself.

Sirens suddenly lit up the exit area. Three units converged under a green sign filled with arrows directing drivers to different highways.

The cab slowed and stopped. Sarah kept running. With one backward glance, she saw Kierian and Clint following her at a good pace.

The cab's driver's side door opened. Then the back door. The little girl scrambled out and ran over to a policewoman, where she was promptly led away. Officers moved in closer.

Sarah was within earshot to hear them order the man out of the vehicle's back seat. He came out sans backpack, both hands on his head.

Sarah slowed and leaned on a pillar to catch her breath. Kierian came up behind her. Between breaths, he congratulated her.

"Well done, Sarah," he said. "I believe you now."

"Believe?"

"Yeah, in you." He panted for a few breaths. "Not Vivian."

"Whatever." She turned from him and watched as the man was placed in the back seat of a cruiser. "That's not what this was about."

"Yeah, sure."

"What about that bomb-sniffing dog and handler thing I told you about? You going to hire one for the end of the week?"

"Yeah, sure. But not here. We can call that sort of thing in."

Kierian's phone rang. "Kierian here."

He paused, listening. "Are you serious?" he said into the

phone. Another pause. "Yes, she's still with us."

Sarah gave him a look wanting to know who he was talking to.

"Okay, I'll bring her right over." He clicked his phone off and dropped it in his pocket.

"You're not going to believe this," he said.

"What? Tell us." She looked at Clint, who had gotten his breath back.

"The Leap Year Killer fucked up."

"How?"

"Two of his victims were just discovered in a cage in the basement of an old warehouse off a street called Keele somewhere in northern Toronto."

"What? How? Who just called you?"

"That was Lyson. Apparently, a worker from another business across the street had gotten suspicious about abnormal activity and went in to investigate. He had to be seen by medics as well."

They started walking back to their car.

"Why? Did he surprise the killer?"

"No. A colleague of his saw him enter the building. He followed him in to see what he was doing. Scared him so bad he fainted and banged his head hard."

Clint chimed in. "So the hero got hurt?"

"Exactly," Kierian said. "You're familiar with that, aren't you, Sarah?"

She didn't reply.

They entered the sliding doors to go back to the car through the airport, where it was warmer.

Sarah looked over her shoulder, a sudden movement by a ledge in the parking area across the street catching her eye.

She looked away and kept walking. Just before they passed another window, she snapped her head sideways and looked at the same spot.

She was sure she saw the face of the AOV member from the coffee shop before he ducked down out of sight.

Chapter 24

SARAH SAT IN THE back seat of the Impala as it warmed up while Kierian and Clint dealt with airport security. After ten minutes with the car's heater on full, she was about to lean into the front seat to turn the heater down when both doors opened, and the FBI men jumped in simultaneously.

Kierian spun around in his seat to address Sarah. "The girl called home to talk to her mother. When her mother got on the phone, she apologized for lying and said she wanted to go home. The perp had said he was nineteen and rich. He has a long list of priors." Kierian turned back around and patted Clint on the shoulder. "We did good, guys."

"I'm not a guy," Sarah said. "And we didn't do anything. We almost lost him. That was too close."

As Kierian drove away from the airport, Sarah wondered if she should tell them what she saw.

Would the Angels of Violence attack two FBI agents to

get to me?

Something told her they would.

She turned to see if they were being followed. The back window had frosted over, the defroster still working to clear it.

"Sarah, you all right?" Kierian asked.

"Yeah."

"What's got your interest behind us?"

She decided it was better they knew. "Thought I saw those AOV guys."

"Really? Here? You think they're following us?"

"They said they had a debt to settle."

"They aren't going to collect while you're with us," Kierian assured her.

"Are you sure about that?" Sarah asked. "Because what you said in the coffee shop ..."

"You're with us. We're trained agents. If anybody tries anything, we'll arrest them. Nothing's going to happen."

"I wasn't looking for reassurance. They're here. I'm sure I saw one of them watching us. Just thought you should know."

Kierian smiled at her in the mirror.

Asshole.

She dropped down in the seat, tired after a long day of adrenaline and exhausting talks. At least she was wearing a sweater now. She had left the skimpy top in the bathroom garbage at the airport.

They drove past the assembled police cars, swung up on a high ramp, and followed it to the 427, heading south toward the downtown area. She didn't look out the back window again because Kierian was using his rearview mirror enough for the both of them.

She almost fell asleep before they turned off the Gardiner Expressway for Yonge Street.

"I need a coffee when we get out," she said, happy this day was almost over.

Kierian parked two blocks farther from the police station than before, the coffee shop they had talked in earlier a block away on her left.

They got out and met on the sidewalk.

"Clint, you want a coffee, too?" Kierian asked.

He nodded. Sarah wondered why he didn't talk much. Was he intimidated in front of women?

They passed an alley. Sarah's hand numbed.

"Guys. Stop."

"What?" Kierian turned back. "Something wrong?"

Her arm numbed. "Got something to write with?"

Kierian touched his pockets. Clint did the same. "I have a pen, but my pad is in the car."

Her other hand numbed. "Oh shit. I think you had better run."

"Why?" Kierian stepped closer. "You're pale, Sarah. What's happening?"

"This isn't a message to write something. Vivian is warning me that danger …" She looked over her shoulder. Then down the alley.

Nothing moved.

The numbness left instantly. She flexed her fingers. "She's trying to tell me something—" The numbing struck with a suddenness she had never felt before. She could barely open her mouth to scream, paralyzed by the sudden control of her muscles.

Then her voice worked. "Run!"

Both men stepped back at her outburst but didn't move.

Then Kierian looked past Sarah and had his sidearm out in under a second. Clint did the same.

"FBI. Step back," Kierian ordered. "Final warning."

The numbness left her limbs. She turned to see what the FBI men were looking at.

Four AOV members with facial tattoos were ten feet behind Sarah. In the alley, four more materialized. When she looked back at Kierian and Clint, there were six behind them.

The steel tip of a long-barreled gun edged along Kierian's shoulder and lightly touched the bottom of his jaw. The same happened to Clint.

Kierian's face relaxed, his expression one of failure.

The man to Sarah's right spoke first. "Drop your weapons, ese. Then move into the alley. We're only here to talk."

"You know as well as I do that we will not give up our guns," Kierian said. "The first wrong move by your people, I shoot you first."

"Then we will both die." The man spat on the pavement and moved closer. "You think I care?" He stepped up to Kierian's weapon and placed his chest on the tip, his face a chunk of solid stone. "You think a member of the Angels of Violence is scared away by a threat of violence?" He leaned in closer. "You don't know who we are, do you?"

Sarah stepped back. There were too many to fight. Aaron had taught her how to fight three, four, and even five men at once, but not fourteen. They were all lean, strong, tattooed, and angry. None of them were dressed for the weather.

"Kill me," the man said, "and my men will pump every

bullet they've got in your face. Then I will have those four," he paused as the four in the alley moved out into the streetlight's glow, each carrying a machete, "tear your arms and legs off and feed them to you." He tilted his head. "Then we find out where you live, pig, and do the same to your family."

"Okay, take it easy," Kierian said without dropping his weapon. "We are federal agents—"

"Who are a long way from home. Try to arrest me," the man said, holding his hands up together as if inviting handcuffs. "Now stop wasting time and give me your weapons."

The steel against Kierian's jaw jabbed harder, pushing his head sideways.

Kierian raised his weapon and clicked the safety on. Clint did the same.

The man took each weapon and stepped back. "Take them in the alley to talk."

Arms grabbed Sarah and dragged her backward so fast she couldn't get a foothold. Kierian and Clint each had three men on them. Ten feet into the alley, which was only lit by a small light from behind what appeared to be a restaurant, Clint and Kierian were knocked off their feet. They fell hard to the cold concrete of the alley.

"Hurt them," the leader ordered.

"No," Sarah said. "What is this all about? You got me. What do you want?"

Their leader turned to her and walked over in three long strides. Two men still held her arms.

"Shut up, bitch," he said quietly. She didn't see his hand coming in the dark alley until it was too late. It connected with the side of her face so hard the man on her right almost lost his grip when she twisted from the hit. The sting was instant, the anger faster.

"You motherfu—"

Another open-palmed slap struck the words out of her mouth. She tasted blood. Her eyes swam.

"One more word out of your pussy mouth, and the pain you feel will be my pleasure."

Sarah hung suspended by her arms, collecting herself and her thoughts. It would do no good to be held up by a man on each arm and beaten. With every hit, her chance of escape dwindled.

The sound of flesh being kicked filled the alley. She watched as four men stomped on each FBI agent with their boots. Both men grunted, groaned, and rolled into a ball, but that didn't matter. The gang members kicked at their lower backs, groins, faces, and heads.

"You're going to kill them," Sarah pleaded.

The man's hand came back too fast again. She tried to duck out of the way but didn't make it. His fingers whipped across her cheeks, his nails cutting into her.

The stomping in front of her stopped. One of the men with a machete walked up to Clint. He was unconscious, bleeding from so many places his face was a mask of red.

"The FBI in Canada, eh?" one of the men with the machetes said. "Yeah, right. Fuckin' poser." He drew the machete along the front of Clint's neck, slicing so deep Clint's head rolled back as his body spasmed and jerked.

"Noooo!" Sarah yelled. She couldn't believe what she was watching. "You can't—what are you doing?" she screamed, struggling against the arms that held her.

He ignored her outburst as he stepped up to Kierian, who was also unconscious and covered in blood.

"Hey, what's going on?" someone asked from the mouth of the alley. A flashlight lit them up. "What are you doing?"

"Go," the leader ordered. "Scramble."

"Police, freeze. Get back here."

Sarah was lifted off the ground and carried to the end of the alley as a tear for Clint slipped down her cheek. Shock settled over her system.

Then they were around the corner and onto a new street. A van door slid open, and Sarah was airborne. She landed inside the van hard and twisted her wrist.

She spun around and got on all fours, ready to dive out of the open door, but men jumped in, blocking her way. The door slammed shut, and the van took off. A boot to the stomach knocked her against the wall.

The van was going faster now.

Another boot came down and blocked the light, connecting with her forehead.

A blessed unconsciousness took over.

Chapter 25

His patience ran thin, Aaron left his apartment and headed to the police station where Alan Lyson worked. Sarah had called and said she would be home. Russell had called and warned him. Someone else had called but, after asking for Sarah, had hung up.

Something bigger than what was in Vivian's messages was happening, and Aaron had a bad vibe that Sarah was in serious trouble and needed his help.

Half an hour later, a few blocks from the station, he came upon a cordoned-off area by an alleyway. Lights flashed from the tops of emergency vehicles lighting the night up in multi-colored strobes, reflecting off the glass of nearby buildings.

He drew closer and mixed in with the small crowd braving the cold to watch the action beyond the police tape.

"What's going on?" he asked the man to his right. "Did you see anything?"

"Not sure. Just got here myself, but I heard a cop might have been killed. Someone came out of that alley on a stretcher, their face covered in a blanket."

Stones weighed down Aaron's stomach. "Who could do such a thing?"

"I know," the man said. "City's gone to shit."

Aaron worked around the crowd and the taped-off area and continued down the sidewalk to the police building.

Sarah had better not have been a part of that, or there'll be shit to pay.

He entered the station and walked up to the front desk.

"Help you?" a female clerk asked.

"I'm here to speak with Detective Lyson."

"I'll ring him." The woman picked up a phone and punched a few buttons. She held the phone away and said, "Name?"

"Aaron Stevens. He'll know me."

The woman whispered into the phone and then set it down. Aaron raised his eyebrows, waiting for a response.

"He'll be down in a moment. You can wait over there." She gestured to a row of chairs.

Aaron left the counter but didn't sit. He was too anxious, too stirred up. Maybe he needed to call Daniel, Alex, and Benjamin, his friends, and fellow teachers at the dojo. The foursome could solve whatever was going on like they did in Greece when Clive Baron had killed Aaron's sister.

He was done with assholes taking the women he cared about from him. Not Sarah. This was not happening again.

"Aaron," a male voice spoke softly behind him.

He spun around and looked into the eyes of Alan Lyson. He lowered his head but kept his eyes on Lyson. "What's happening? Tell me what you know."

"Come to my office."

On the stairs, Lyson said, "I read the file on you before I came to visit your apartment the other night."

"Interesting reading?" Aaron asked.

"Very. What I found interesting was your abilities and your dogged determination to deal with who had hurt your sister."

"That hasn't diminished. I will find Sarah."

They reached the second landing, and Lyson turned for the hall.

"Of that," he said, "I have little doubt. Is everyone attached to Sarah such vigilantes?"

Aaron ignored the question.

A man sat on a couch against the back wall in Lyson's office.

"That's Justin," Lyson said. "He's a member of the task force set up to locate the man I asked Sarah to help us find."

Aaron nodded at Justin, then turned to Lyson. "How's that going?"

"We can't talk police business with a member of the public."

Aaron frowned. "Then why bring me to your office to update me and then say nothing?"

"I didn't say update."

Aaron looked at Justin. He could have both men on the floor within six seconds. One would be unconscious, and the other would be begging to tell him what was going on. But he didn't want to spend the next ten years in prison. Or upset Sarah.

"Look," Aaron said in a calm voice. "Maybe I can help.

Bring me in on this.”

“How could you help?” Lyson asked.

It began to feel that that was exactly what Lyson had been waiting for.

“I want something in return,” Aaron said.

“What’s that?” Lyson crossed his arms and waited.

“I want a ride-along.”

“A ride-along?” Lyson smiled. “What are we talking about here?”

“I offer what I know. You keep me up to date on what’s happening with Sarah. She’s all I’ve got. You don’t want me on the street with my guys doing this on our own. We’ve had too much of that. Deal?”

Lyson rubbed the bottom of his chin in an exaggerated display of contemplation. He looked like he was enjoying this. Then it clicked. When Lyson came to his apartment and asked for help, he got kicked out.

Now Aaron needed him. The difference here was that Lyson actually *did* need Aaron.

“Goodbye,” Aaron said without waiting for a response. He turned for the door, walked across the small office, and grabbed the handle.

“Wait.”

He stopped.

“You have a deal.”

He turned around. “Full disclosure. I want everything. In exchange, I’m yours. Everything I know about Sarah’s ability. Deal?”

“Deal.” Lyson nodded.

Justin nodded as well.

“Tell me,” Aaron said as he walked back in front of

Lyson's desk. "What's going on?"

"I guess I could say it's not going well."

"Why do you guess?"

Lyson sat behind his desk. Aaron remained standing, his hands clasped together in front of him, legs spread.

"What I'm about to tell you isn't public knowledge. I'm willing to go out on a limb and let you in on what's happening. But it doesn't leave this room. Clear?"

"Clear."

"Two intended victims of The Leap Year Killer were freed earlier tonight."

"Did Sarah have anything to do with this?"

Lyson shook his head. "No. A worker from a building across the street discovered them in a cage."

"Where's Sarah?"

"We don't know." Lyson looked at Justin on the couch. "We didn't fuck up. It has nothing to do with us."

"What do you mean?" Aaron asked, trying hard to keep his temper in check.

"The FBI stormed in here and left with her hours ago. My understanding is that they went to the Toronto airport."

"The airport?" he almost shouted.

"There was an arrest, a man Sarah and the FBI stopped —"

"The luring thing. Yeah, I know about that. He tried to steal a thirteen-year-old girl."

Another exchange of looks between the task force members. Aaron turned to address Justin. "I read the notes Vivian gave Sarah. She shared them with me."

Lyson leaned forward and rested his forearms on his large desk calendar. "All of them?"

Aaron nodded. "Most of it."

"Tell us what Vivian has been saying?"

"I only saw the massage parlor thing and then the airport one. There was one more note, but I didn't see all of it. There was an address and a time to be there." He thought for a second. "Something about keeping the building clear of all police personnel, too."

"You remember a lot for a note you didn't see much of."

"I glanced at it, saw the address, the date, and then a bunch of text. The words *police* and *building clear* stood out, but I didn't read it."

"Can you remember the specific address or the date?" Lyson asked.

"Leap day."

"What did the address have to do with that date?"

"Tell me where Sarah is?" Aaron countered.

"We don't know," Lyson said as he leaned back in his chair. "I already told you that."

Aaron unzipped his jacket as the heat in the office overcame him. "What happened a block from here?"

"Two FBI agents were attacked."

"They okay?"

"One of them is in the hospital. The other ..." he shook his head. "Fucking tragedy."

"Wouldn't happen to be the same two FBI guys from last night, would it? The same two that took Sarah to the airport?" He was putting it together, and every which way it shaped up, things did not look good for Sarah.

Lyson's grim face looked away. "Unfortunately."

"And that's why you don't know where she is?"

Lyson nodded.

"Why do I have to drag this out of you? Fuck." He turned around and paced the floor to the door and back. "What are the two victims you recovered saying?"

"Nothing. They can't talk."

Aaron frowned and turned his head sideways. "More dragging shit out of you? So tell me, why can't they talk?"

"The killer removed their tongues."

"What? And you guys let Sarah deal with hardened criminals like that?"

Lyson stood from his chair. "Let's get one thing straight. *We* don't *let* Sarah do anything. She does what she wants. The only help we ask is if she can do a message thing and tell us something we don't know."

"Well, your little helper sounds helpless right now."

"The blame is not in this office—"

The phone on his desk rang. Lyson picked it up. "I thought I said I didn't want to be disturbed." A pause, then his voice softened. "Right, okay, put her through."

He clicked speaker phone.

"Hello?" a woman's voice.

"Maria, you're on speaker with Justin and Aaron Stevens."

"Aaron?"

"You remember Aaron, Sarah's guy? He might be able to help. He has an address he's trying to remember. Maybe something you say will help him."

"I just finished at the crisis center."

"And?"

"That woman we were looking into, Jennifer, is pretty shaken up."

"Why's that? I know her. She's been there a long time,

like maybe a decade or longer. Good girl."

"Do you know who her brother is?"

"No idea. Didn't even know she had a brother."

"His name is Martin Rankin, the medical examiner working this Leap Year Killer case."

"What? Really?" Lyson's eyes bulged a little.

"She can't get a hold of him."

"So?"

"One of the women recovered in the cage had visited Jennifer last week."

"And?"

Aaron stepped closer to the desk to listen better, nervous for Sarah because she had just gone to the crisis center and spoken to a woman named Jennifer.

"When I told Jennifer the names of the other six victims and showed her their pictures, she was the only employee who had been there long enough to know them all. Sometimes she complains about her job to her brother even though case files are confidential."

"It could be construed that Jennifer is the common denominator and not Martin." Lyson sounded like he was thinking out loud. "That alone does not make anyone a murderer."

"I tried calling our medical examiner today but can't get to him. He's not answering his cell or his home line. No one's seen Martin Rankin for at least twenty-four hours."

"What does he drive?"

"A Range Rover, the same color and make as our witness said, was parked out front of that abandoned warehouse. I suspect it's the same Range Rover that Martin drives."

"Sounds like you're on to something," Lyson said as he

brushed a hand through his hair. "That's our ME," he said, almost to himself. "He's been with us for years without a single red flag."

"Hide in plain sight, sir. Ted Bundy."

"Okay, we'll find him and bring him in."

Lyson hung up and turned to Justin. "Do what you can to locate our medical examiner." He turned back to Aaron. "Was there anything else?"

"Yes. Russell called."

"Who is Russell?"

"Sarah's cousin."

"What did he want?"

"He had a warning."

"A warning?"

"He said it all ends with fire or bombs, and Sarah won't make it. She's too determined to do the right thing, he said. It's what'll kill her in the end."

Someone knocked on the door.

"So much for do not disturb," Lyson muttered. "Hold on, Aaron. I want to hear more."

A uniformed officer entered, walked over to Lyson's desk, and handed him a sealed envelope. "For you, sir. It just arrived at the front desk."

Lyson took it and examined the envelope as the officer retreated. "Just my name."

He set the envelope on the desk and pulled gloves out of a drawer. Using tweezers in each hand, he slit the envelope open and pulled the paper out. After reading it, he gestured for Justin to come to his desk and read it, too.

"What?" Aaron asked. "What does it say?"

"Looks like our serial killer wants to meet me on leap

day just before midnight at the building where he had his victims caged."

"What for?" Aaron asked, feeling out of his depth.

"Probably wants to kill me."

Justin added, "The note says the building should be cleared of all police personnel. If even one officer other than Lyson is within a mile of the building, the meeting will not occur, and our killer will disappear."

"Building cleared?" Aaron said. "Sounds like Sarah's note. Wait. Is this building on Keele Street?"

Both officers looked at each other and then back at Aaron.

They nodded.

"That's it. Same as Sarah's note. Vivian said it ends there."

Justin looked down at the note again. "The perp says he wants to surrender but will only surrender to Lyson." Justin stared at the page a moment longer. "Did you read the bottom?" He looked at Lyson.

"I did."

"What's the bottom say?" Aaron asked.

"It says Lyson has to bring one other person with him, or the surrender deal is off."

"Who?" Aaron asked but already knew the answer.

"Sarah Roberts."

Chapter 26

Someone shouted. Loud music vibrated the floor.

Her arms were on fire. The ache was so intense she dared not move lest she screamed in pain.

Sarah opened her eyes to a slit and took in the room. The bits of furniture were ruined. Holes littered a couch; the fabric pulled up like a large dog used it as a chew toy. The small doors of a cabinet against the back wall had broken glass still attached to the door's frame. Garbage was strewn about. A red McDonald's fries container, ripped candy bar sleeve, gum packages, and cigarette boxes. It looked like a crack house. It was musky and smelled like a dank cottage that hadn't been opened in years.

Her hands were bound by chains bolted into a brick wall. They were suspended above her head, white in the sunlight filtering through the stained sheet they used as a curtain.

Sunlight? She must've been out since last night. It all

came back to her in a torrent. Kierian was lying on the concrete, knocked out, blood everywhere. Clint's throat being sliced open like a watermelon.

She shuddered, pain running along her arms. She wanted to cry for them but couldn't. She needed to get out of here first. Stay alive now, and grieve later.

She probed her mouth with her tongue and felt her teeth where they were supposed to be. Her bottom lip had swollen from the slaps, but the side of her face hurt the most. That boot had come down hard and fast. It must've rammed the other side of her face into the van's floor. She could have a concussion and shouldn't be sleeping, but she doubted her captors would care.

What did they have planned for her if she was still alive? Killing an FBI agent could bring every cop in North America after them. Maybe that was why they had kept her alive. To serve as a hostage.

The thumping music quieted as the song changed and then started up again. Her head pounded with it.

Someone walked by the door to the living room-like area they had her suspended in. They peeked in at her.

"Hey!" he shouted. "Turn that shit down. You woke the bitch up."

He stepped into the room. The music died. Footsteps ran down the hall toward her room. Tattooed men filed in, one after another, until there were at least fifteen of them.

The alpha male weaved through to the front.

"Do you know why you're here?" he asked.

"Hostage?" she mumbled through her dry mouth. "Negotiate with the police?"

He turned to his gang members and laughed, holding his

stomach.

"You hold yourself in high regard. No, you are not our hostage. You are our prisoner. We don't negotiate with anybody. Do you know why that is?"

"No," Sarah whispered. Talking made her headache flare. The pain in her shoulders was so constant they had gone numb.

"You're here because you shot one of ours in the leg."

"That asshole at the massage parlor?"

He stepped close enough that his breath caressed her skin. He wrapped his large hands around each of her breasts and squeezed from outside her sweater.

"Ripe peaches here," he said. "Ripe for the taking."

He continued to squeeze until Sarah couldn't contain her pain-filled moan. His hands tightened into fists, her breasts caught in the trap of his palm.

She screamed.

"That's right," he yelled loud enough to be heard over her. "Scream bitch, scream."

He dug in harder if that were possible.

A few of the men behind him cheered and shouted, egging him on.

Sarah screamed and pulled on the chains that bound her. It felt like her breasts were literally being torn from her body as her head threatened to explode in pain.

Her legs were not secured. It took everything in her to keep her feet rooted. Thoughts of wrapping her legs around the man's waist and locking him in the scissor hold Aaron had taught her. The asshole wouldn't be able to breathe as she assaulted his diaphragm. Another thought was to kick him in the groin hard enough to send his balls into his neck.

But lifting her legs meant all her weight would drop onto her arms which were already numb with pain. Even if she tried to fight, she would never leave this building alive.

The pressure on her chest eased. The man dropped his hands to his side and stepped back.

Her screaming was replaced with moaning as the pain subsided. Slowly.

"Insult one of us again, and I will remove your tits with a knife. I understand women can still live wonderful lives with no fucking tits. Don't test my patience. I don't have any."

Sarah mumbled.

"What was that?"

"I'm sorry," Sarah said, realizing that she would have to manage these people as best she could if she intended to walk away from this as a whole person. She understood people like this. Only fight back when there are three or less and fight to kill. Hurting these men, even breaking a bone, would only anger them further.

He didn't acknowledge her apology.

"You're here because the man you shot wants his revenge. That's what we do for each other. He should be out of his holding cell within a few days. Then he will come here and make you pay for what you did to him."

"Can I have some water?"

He motioned for one of the men to leave the room and fetch water. Then he turned to the assembled gang. "Everyone, go back to what you were doing. We're going to talk in here. I want you all out."

A few moments later, the leader and Sarah were alone in the living room. Her breathing normalized as the pain in her chest and head dulled. No doubt the bruises would look horrible.

Just wait until Aaron sees it.

"Do you know why Juan was after that whore at the massage parlor?"

Sarah shook her head.

"Because she wanted into AOV. Have you heard of us?"

"Those men in the alley told me."

"The Angels of Violence. Respect that."

Sarah looked away. She wanted to tear him apart but was paralyzed as long as her arms were locked behind her.

He pulled the sheet aside to look out the window. "You know, people from all over North America want to join AOV."

"I didn't know that."

He dropped the sheet back in place and leaned against the wall by the window, examining a fingernail. The first two knuckles were bloody and crusted over with scabs. He had two cuts on each forearm and at least three scars on his face and forehead. Just looking at him, his build, and his tats, she could tell he was a brawler, a street fighter.

"We have over seventy-thousand members in the States, Mexico, and now Canada. Think of us as tailor-made for urban terrorism for hire. Killing cops is a good business—our specialty." He pushed off the wall and paced in front of her. "We engraved the name of a pig on a bullet and left it on his doorstep. We almost always locate any witnesses who even think to testify against us and execute them." He stopped pacing and stepped close, his eyes black. He smiled in a feral way. "We protect turf, our members, and our cash with our lives. Do you understand?"

"Yes," Sarah said.

"That is why you are here. You hurt one of us even though he betrayed the unit."

"Betrayed?"

"We have initiation rites to become one of us."

A man entered with water and brought it to Sarah. It was in an empty Coke bottle with a straw. Tap water. She didn't care, drinking hard and fast. It reminded her she had to pee but wasn't going to do it in front of any of these men.

The bottle was pulled away, and the man left the room.

"To become a member of AOV, the first initiation is called Walk The Line. You must commit an extremely violent act against an innocent victim, such as a severe beating, a violent rape, or murder." He moved to her left, keeping his eyes on her.

She decided if he touched her again, she probably wouldn't be able to control herself. She would attack with the intent to kill, just like Aaron had taught her.

Screw the consequences. This man isn't human.

"The second rite is called Jump In. That can be terrifying for most. Five of our strongest members beat the recruit to a pulp for fifteen seconds. The rest stand back and count to fifteen. We start the recruiting age at nine years old. Laws in Canada don't charge anyone under twelve. See the math?"

Sarah nodded.

"We get our recruits under twelve to perform as many execution orders as we can because they can't be processed in the system."

He checked the hallway. Then he walked to her side.

"In one instance, I watched a ten-year-old boy placed in a circle of five large men and then get stomped on. After fifteen seconds, there wasn't much left of him. Sometimes members don't make it through initiation. But that's what it's for."

It had to be untrue. Could AOV be that animalistic? She had heard similar things in the past and listened to the news of what the drug cartels had done in South America, but she had never met a gang so brutal that nothing humane mattered.

Nothing scared these people. Not even cops.

"The third rite is for girls who want to join. It's called, Sexed In. They must endure a gang rape by at least fifteen members in one hour, and it has to be violent." He moved to her other side. "That girl you tried to save at the massage parlor had a bruised face. Mostly around the eyes. Do you remember?"

Sarah nodded.

"And she left a statement with the police blaming everything on you?"

Sarah nodded again.

"She knew to protect Juan, her man. If she didn't, she wouldn't make the night. Betrayal is the worst crime and is dealt with most brutally." He raised his index finger. "But we are getting off track. Juan's woman was set to handle her initiation. We got started, but she fought back after only three members had pumped her. Juan was at the parlor to bring her back here to finish her initiation, and you fucked that up. Do you know what that means?"

"No," Sarah muttered, sure it meant this man was going to kill her now while she was tied up and unable to defend herself.

"It means when Juan gets out of jail in a few days, you have to do the initiation rite for the girl you saved, starting with Juan. And since you shot him, and he's really upset about that, you may not survive the first gang banger of the fifteen men who are to pump you hard." He leaned in close and smiled. "Do you think you'll enjoy that, tough girl?"

She raised her face and met his eyes. They were dark orbs of hate.

"Tell Juan I'm waiting. Bring it on."

He laughed as he walked to the door.

"After Juan, you will be fucked by Death."

"That'll ruin it for the rest of the fifteen," she said, not caring anymore.

"My name is Death. That is the name I got when I entered AOV because of all the people I had killed." He smiled like he was proud of murder. "When Juan is done with you, I get you. When I'm done, nothing will be left of you."

He walked away, his laughter echoing down the hall, trailing him in blackness.

Chapter 27

BY THE TIME LYSON had made a dozen calls and got Aaron in his cruiser, it was nearly two in the morning. He had instructed everyone on the task force and the crime-scene technicians to finish what they were doing double time and get out of that warehouse on Keele Street. It was to be roped off, and no one would be allowed to enter the building again until the first of March.

"I might even get a makeshift fence constructed around the exterior to seal it off," Lyson said.

"How do you know the letter was actually from the Leap Year Killer?" Aaron asked.

"It's at the lab being analyzed right now. But this is the second one. Same stationery, same envelope, same cursive handwriting. The odds are higher than ninety percent it's our guy."

The streets were quiet at this late hour on a cold February

evening. Even Highway 401, a usually bustling stop-and-go parking lot in the day, was nearly empty. They took the Keele Street exit and headed north.

"You want coffee?" Aaron asked.

"Sure. I'll pull over up here at the Timmy's."

They took two to go and got back in the car. Lyson sat and sipped from his cup without starting the car.

"What happened with that cop Folley and your sister's case?" Lyson asked.

Aaron turned away and stared out the window. "Folley was a good cop when he wanted to be. Found my parents for me even though I didn't want him to."

"What do you mean 'when he wanted to be'?"

"He found my parents but couldn't find my sister when it counted. Although, even if he had, it would've been too late."

Lyson set his cup in the holder. "Was your sister one of the bodies recovered in Casa Loma?"

Aaron nodded.

"I'm sorry."

"Things are better. It's been a couple of years now. How about you? What's your story?"

"Near retirement. Next month. This'll be my last case."

Aaron set his coffee down. "Wife? Kids? Golf?"

Now it was Lyson's turn to look outside and stare at nothing. He turned the car on to combat the cold that was seeping in.

"Married once. No kids."

"What happened?"

"She died."

"Sorry."

Lyson shook his head. "It happens. Routine stop. My

wife and her partner pulled over a drunk driver high on something. They got out. Followed procedures and asked the driver to exit the vehicle. He didn't."

"What happened?"

"He hit the gas instead."

"Surely she wasn't standing in front of the car?" Aaron asked.

"No, no. She was on the side. The driver squealed away, spun the wheel hard to the left, and did a U-turn in front of them. They were running for their cruiser. He rammed them, doing at least fifty. Knocked himself out with the airbag."

"And that killed her?"

"No, just stunned her. She got out, walked around the other car, her gun drawn, and ordered the driver out. The problem was they were on the side of a two-lane highway during the evening. Her cruiser's lights and parking lights were knocked out when the other vehicle smashed the battery and engine block of the cruiser. The perp's car was off, no lights. She had a flashlight, but that was it."

"Oh, no ..."

Lyson nodded. "A semi came along, and didn't see anything until it was too late. He jerked on the wheel and cleared both vehicles with his cab, but the trailer was overweight. It tipped and slid sideways, smashing the trunk of the cruiser first and working its way through the drunk's car. It hit Caroline last, decapitating her. They found her head in the ditch thirty feet away from her body." He turned to look at Aaron; his eyes rimmed with wetness. "Her gun was still in her hand."

"Tough lady."

"You got that right," Lyson said and dropped the vehicle

into gear. "We've still got a lot of work to do tonight. Let's go make sure that everything is done at the warehouse, and then I'll take you home."

"Home? I'm not going home."

"I am. We have to sleep. We can't work twenty-four hours a day to save people. We have to eat and sleep."

"Isn't there anything I could do to help?"

"Actually, there is. Go home and sleep. In two days, we're giving you a ride-along. We're raiding known street gang hideouts. We'll find Sarah and then get her to this meeting with the Leap Year Killer so we can nail him, too. Once he's off the streets, you and Sarah can go back to your lives."

"Somehow, I don't think it'll be that easy."

Chapter 28

THREE DAYS HAD PASSED without much happening. They had taken her down from the wall, tying her to a longer chain. She was still manacled, but now her limbs weren't suspended above her. It had taken all of a day for the feeling to come back to what she considered normal.

They fed her decently and gave her enough water to never be thirsty. But no shower. Not even a wet cloth.

Death came and talked to her frequently throughout the day. No one was allowed in her room but him. He had posted a large, tattooed man as a sentry who was given breaks by a wiry youth no older than sixteen.

Sarah had devised a few escape plans, but all of them involved the chains not being on her wrists. So far, they had only removed them to hook on the longer links. She had to use a bucket as a toilet. At least they gave her privacy for that.

Presently, the sun was high, and the house quiet. Throughout the day, most of them were doing whatever it was street gangs that did. If she were ever going to get out of here, it would have to be the daytime.

"Hey?" she called to the guy sitting just outside her door.

He didn't move.

"Hey? Think I could get something to read? Pretty boring in here."

"You're not here to be entertained. You wait. Your time is coming."

"I know that. Just thought maybe I could read while I wait. Like at a dentist or doctor's office."

He peeked around the doorframe, a sneer on his face, then looked away.

"When do you think Juan is coming? This is getting boring."

"Soon enough. You'll regret you asked that when he gets here."

"He's going to be pissed at you guys when he gets here. Not just me."

"Yeah? Why's that?" The guy looked around the edge again.

"Because I haven't had a shower in three days. You've left me chained to a wall. You think he's gonna want to have a piece of this smelling the way I do?"

"You're so stupid," he said and looked away. "No more talking."

"Why am I stupid? Seems rational to me. Let me take a shower."

"You're not showering because Juan likes it dirty. He's the sickest one of all of us. Remember, it was his woman that he offered fifteen of us to beat on as we violated her. He wanted to go last. Do you think he's worried about your body odor? Classy bitch."

This gang qualified for the worst humans she had ever met. They all deserved to either die or be in prison for the rest of their lives. There couldn't be a reform for this kind of criminal.

"Can't say I've been called a classy bitch before."

"No more talking."

"Yeah," a voice boomed from the front of the house. Death was home. "No more talking!"

He stomped through the house and entered the living room. Fresh blood smeared his hands.

"What happened to you?" Sarah asked.

"Rival gang. Wrong territory. Didn't read the signs on the way in. Learned to read today." He turned to the sentry posted at the door. "Take a break."

The guy got up and walked away. A door slammed somewhere deep in the house. Death wiped his hands on his pants and yanked the sentry's chair from the hall. He straddled it backward and sat down facing Sarah.

"We have a problem," he said.

"What's that?" Sarah asked, not really wanting to hear the answer.

"I like air. I enjoy watching things fly."

She had gotten used to talking to Death. His name wasn't all that original. He was big on honor and doing right by the gang. And he loved killing a little too much. His views on things were twisted.

"Planes are nice." Her tone wasn't patronizing. "Go to an airport. Watch them fly."

"I like watching things fly that don't have wings."

"What, like skateboarders, motorcyclists doing jumps?"

"Close. I'm talking about unnatural flight."

"Okay," she said, even though she had no idea where he was going.

"I've killed a lot of people. Young and old, male and female."

She stayed silent. Sentences like that made her want to pummel him, break a few bones in his face and wait for the police to take him to prison. How Death was still in society was beyond her. It only reminded her of how many truly sick individuals walked among the general public every day without anyone knowing who they were.

"But I have never *thrown* anyone off a building before. I want to see that. I want to see someone die from flight."

"Interesting."

"And I want that to be you," he said, pointing at her. "I am going to take you to the top of a building somewhere and throw you off. How's that?"

"I'm not afraid of heights," she said. He leaned back and smiled. "I'm not afraid of falling, either. It's that sudden stop at the end. That's a real bitch."

He dropped his hand and stared at her. "That was a joke, right? I get it. Good one." He stood and moved the chair aside. "I've decided. Tomorrow night. I will throw you off a building. Then you die."

He headed for the door.

"Juan's going to be pissed. Isn't he coming for me?"

Death turned at the door. "He's being released tomorrow afternoon. His lawyer has secured that. We'll be picking him up. But he won't be upset that he misses out on you."

"Why's that? Doesn't he want his revenge?"

"You haven't been listening. We have a party when one of us is released from prison, but we can't have that party here. Too much attention. This has become a fortified clubhouse in the woods. We'll locate a building, have a party, deal with Juan, and then I'll throw you off the roof." He smiled wide, his crazy look mastered. "Once, a long time ago, we were featured in National Geographic as one of the world's most dangerous gangs. Even Newsweek did a feature on AOV. We're famous for knives and machetes."

"You've told me some of this."

"I know, but you weren't listening. When one of us tries to stop someone from getting shot or hurt, that's an act of disloyalty. That person must die next and more violently than anything you can imagine. We have to set an example. Better to swallow your conscience or die in a way you didn't even know possible."

She was putting it together. Juan was coming home—to his own funeral for stopping the initiation on his girlfriend. He was never going to get near Sarah. They only had her here to make her pay for what she did to one of theirs. And to make an apparent show of allegiance to Juan while he was in jail.

"When you shot Juan, he was arrested and taken to the hospital. Tomorrow he's out on crutches. We deal with him then. When he's dead and dismembered, I'll deal with you."

"Then let me help."

"Help? How?" He blinked. "Why?"

She could tell he was instantly suspicious of her motivations. She told him the address Vivian had given her. "It's north of the 401 on Keele. Abandoned warehouse. Find a way in. It's over three stories high. Bring me back up if I don't die on the first throw. I could fly twice."

Death laughed, and she laughed along with him. It grated on her nerves.

"You're joking, right?"

"You need somewhere secluded, where no one will know you're there. I've looked at this place. Secluded and in the industrial part of town. After ten or eleven at night, no one will be around. The warehouse is huge," she added, though she hadn't been inside it yet. "Check it out yourself beforehand."

"Why would you help? You're not making sense. You die in the end."

"Because I would rather die from a fall than the alternative with Juan. You have saved me from that hell."

He frowned. "You are strange." He stared at her a moment more. "I don't believe you, but I'm curious." He stepped close and flexed his hands. "I might check this address out. If I see cops or anything out of the ordinary or think it's a trap for even one second, I will come back here and rape you with a machete. Understand?"

She tried hard not to listen to his words. The thoughts that entered her mind were difficult to banish.

"Understood."

He walked away, taking the chair back to the door. A minute later, someone else walked down the hallway and sat down.

The sentry was back on duty.

Chapter 29

AARON'S KNUCKLES TINGLED WITH the need to punch somebody. He couldn't believe how incompetent the police were in handling Sarah's disappearance. Four days had passed, and they had no leads. She could be anywhere by now. Or dead.

Since potential kidnappers had made no demands, they weren't sure if she was still alive. Lyson told him to prepare for the worst since the odds were working against them.

But they didn't know Sarah as he did.

The raids on gang hangouts and known crack houses had gone well, netting dozens of arrests. But there was no sign of Sarah. No one on the street, according to Lyson's task force, had seen or heard of Sarah Roberts.

Earlier today, a member of a violent street gang named Angels of Violence, known by the tattoos on his face, had been seen near the warehouse where Lyson and Sarah were supposed to meet The Leap Year Killer. Martin Rankin, the medical examiner, had been elevated to a person of interest.

When a member of the task force set up across the street had called in to report a street gang member was seen in the area, Lyson told him to stand down. Let him go. Do not be seen, and do not follow him.

"Why not have him followed?" Aaron asked. He stormed into Lyson's office, ready to fight. "You know that AOV members were in the area when those two FBI agents were attacked. And now, one shows up at the warehouse where you and Sarah are supposed to be tonight. Too coincidental for me."

Lyson set his pen down and looked at Aaron over thin glasses that sat on the end of his nose. "That tattooed man got inside the warehouse, toured it, and was seen on the roof. According to Justin, who manned the cameras across the street, the freak reentered the building and left through a hole in the fence at the back. He disappeared after that. We figure he walked through the snow-covered field at the back and used the train tracks to leave the area by another route."

"Right. Back to my original question. Why not have him followed? He's probably the one holding Sarah. That was the purpose of the gang raids a few days ago. Wasn't it?" Aaron rubbed his face in frustration. The police had their own way, which didn't always make sense to him.

"We didn't follow him because the risk of being discovered was too great. If he is holding Sarah, which I suspect he is, and he saw a tail, Sarah wouldn't be there tonight."

"What?" Aaron couldn't believe what he was hearing. "If you followed him, he would lead you to Sarah."

Lyson shook his head. "No, not these guys. They are very good. He would see us following him a mile away and never go back to his clubhouse. Sarah would be lost forever. Providing they're the ones who have her."

"Why not nab him and *make* him talk."

Lyson chuckled. "You think these are the kinds of guys who rat out the others? You think he'll tell us where she is? An Angels of Violence member would rather spend ten years in prison before he would rat one of his own out. I've seen what happens to one of their members when they're caught being disloyal. No, that would never fly."

"You're instilling hope that Sarah is doing well, having spent almost a week with these kinds of people."

"Sorry. It's just reality."

There was a moment of quiet between them. Lyson picked up his pen and continued writing.

"Have you found Rankin? Did anyone go to his house?"

"What is this, Aaron? Twenty questions?" Lyson took his glasses off and set them on the desk. "I've been doing this a long time, you know, cop stuff."

Aaron gestured with his hands. "I'm sorry. I'm worried for Sarah."

"She can take care of herself. If anyone can, Sarah can."

"Look, Lyson, I'm just trying to get up to speed on what's happening. Tonight's the meeting, and you don't have Sarah yet."

"True, but I believe she's going to be there, and she's bringing friends."

"How so?"

"She knows about the warning from Russell. You told her on the phone when she called you. She was given the warehouse address from Vivian and the time. She knows where she needs to be. We think AOV took her because she shot one of theirs, Juan, who we released today. Juan is being watched. So far, no Sarah. We also surmised that the AOV guy who checked out the warehouse earlier was there on advice of Sarah. Somehow he got the address from her. Sarah doesn't know that the Leap Year Killer requested her at the meeting tonight, but she does know that she's supposed to be there because of Vivian and has worked it out somehow with AOV that she is."

"And you don't feel that's stretching things a little?"

"No." Lyson picked up his glasses. "Call it a hunch."

"A bunch of hunches." Aaron looked at the far wall lined with pictures of Lyson shaking hands with other well-dressed men. "What about your medical examiner?"

Lyson looked up at him.

"What?" Aaron said, gesturing with his hands again, his shoulders raised. "I'm just checking."

"We searched his home. Came up empty. If he's been murdering women for twelve years, which I'm beginning to believe he has, he's been very meticulous about it."

"You have all this manpower, all these leads, and yet we don't know where Sarah is, and we're no further ahead in locating the serial killer. What are you going to do if Sarah doesn't show tonight?"

Lyson slammed his hands down on his desk calendar. "I don't know."

"I'm going to the hospital," Aaron said as he got out of his chair.

"Why there?"

"To see if that FBI agent ... what was his name?"

"Kierian."

"To see if Kierian has woken up yet. If not, maybe they can wake him. He saw the people who had taken Sarah. Maybe he'll have a description."

"Look at you. Mister Detective now. You are not going anywhere near that hospital."

"And why not? I can do what the hell I want to."

"Not without me, you're not."

Lyson got out of his chair and walked around his desk. "Let's go." He grabbed his jacket on the way out.

The late afternoon sun was dropping as they drove in silence the few blocks to the hospital.

Seven hours to showtime and still no Sarah. Aaron figured that Lyson was more worried they would miss their opportunity to nab the Leap Year Killer than he was about whether Sarah would show or not.

A man in a suit sat outside Kierian's room reading a newspaper. The FBI had sent up a couple of men after Clint's body was transported south of the border.

The agent examined their ID, nodded, and said they could go in. They entered Kierian's room quietly. When they did, he turned his bandaged head slightly to look at them. Two other men in suits sat by the window, talking quietly.

They're really protecting this guy, Aaron thought.

He stayed back while Lyson moved to the edge of Kierian's bed.

"No one told me you were awake," Lyson said. "How are you feeling?"

"Okay … considering." His mouth barely moved when he talked. "Sarah?"

Lyson shook his head and pursed his lips. "Nothing. No

word."

"I gave my men … a brief statement." Kierian swallowed. "It was AOV who took her. They were watching us. Said something about retribution."

"We figured. Sarah shot one of theirs at the massage studio."

"Do you have any leads?" Kierian asked.

Lyson shook his head. "None."

Aaron stepped closer. "What about that guy at the warehouse?"

"What guy?" Kierian asked. "Warehouse?"

"Long story, but we have a lead on one of the AOV members."

Kierian's eyes watered. "Don't let my partner die for nothing." He gripped Aaron's hand, probably thinking it was Lyson's. "Tell me you'll nail those bastards."

"We're doing our best," Lyson said. "I assure you. We'll get them." He looked at Aaron and then back at Kierian. "We have to go now. When we have anything new, we'll let you know."

"Wait," Kierian said, just loud enough to be heard. "At the airport, Sarah said something about a dog for sniffing out bombs or explosives. I was supposed to get her one. I didn't. Been tied up in here."

"We took care of that," Lyson said. "There's a meeting at a warehouse tonight that Sarah's supposed to be at. Four days ago, I ordered the place swept. We've been watching it since. C-4 had been hidden in the building, but the bomb squad removed it. Nothing is going to blow up tonight, that's for sure. Sarah won't need bomb-sniffing dogs."

Chapter 30

ALL SARAH NEEDED WAS a safe place to land in the snow when Death threw her from the roof if he made it that far. Better to fall three stories into a couple of feet of snow than stay in the building during the explosion or fire. The fact that all Death's AOV members would be inside the building when something happened to it would hopefully rid the world of people that deserved to die for the horrors they had committed.

She had asked Kierian to get a bomb-sniffing dog, but now that Clint was dead and Kierian was probably still hospitalized, she had little hope that the bombs had been taken care of.

Being tied up the way they had her, she had hoped Death's trip to the warehouse went well. If he came back angry because he saw a random cop or worse and thought she'd sent him to a trap, she shuddered at the thought of what he might do.

But when he returned an hour ago and said the building would work perfectly for their little party for Juan, she couldn't believe it. She only had to figure a way out of the building or onto the roof in time.

Her internal clock told her it was at least ten at night. Her wrists ached from constantly having metal wrapped around them. They were red and chafing, raised up, and swelling. She couldn't wait to have them removed. Her face wasn't as sore anymore, and her fat lip had started to heal nicely.

Her energy was high. They had fed her better than she expected. These past few days, she had rested well under Death's protection with no one bothering her.

Most of the gang had left early in the afternoon to pick up Juan, and only Death had returned an hour ago. But she was sure he had left again. The house was quiet. Even the sentry had been pulled from the door.

"Hello?" she called.

No one responded.

What the fuck?

Where would they have gone?

Tonight's meal had been fast food. She wondered what Aaron was going through, having not heard from her for so long. What were the police doing? She had been kidnapped from two federal agents, one of them killed during the process, the other almost killed. Every cop in the country was probably scouring Toronto for the people responsible. If that were the case, then why hadn't they found this place yet?

Death had mentioned this was a backwoods hideout. She wondered how far they were from Toronto. Strategically, it made sense they would maintain a clubhouse out of the city.

Sometimes it was too dangerous to stay on the streets.

A door slammed down the hall. Her stomach twisted.

They're here. This is it.

Someone walked up the hallway slowly, their footfalls heavy, more pronounced.

It didn't sound like Death or any of his men. Too heavy. Unless they changed into winter boots.

A dark shadow filled the doorway. She could see a silhouette of a gun in one hand and a knife in the other. Liquid dripped from the knife.

"Hello, Sarah," the man said. "I'm a friend of Detective Alan Lyson. He sent me to come to pick you up."

Relief swept through her. "What happened to the men guarding me?"

"They're sleeping. They'll be out for a few hours. Enough time for Lyson's men to come and pick them up."

The man entered the dark room and pulled what looked like a key out of his pocket. "I found this on the crazy-looking guy with tattoos on his face." He shook his head. "Tats on the face. Insane if you ask me."

This close up, she could see his gentle face and graying hair. He was in shape and deft with a knife as he spun it around in his hand and slipped it into a sheath. Dark spots covered the cutting edge, but she wasn't sure if it was blood because she didn't get a good enough look in the dim light.

The man dropped down beside her and gently undid her restraints.

"There," he said. "That's better." He stood and stepped back. "Can you walk?"

"Damn right, I can." She got to her feet, both legs shaky from lack of use, and followed him from the room. She hadn't been awake when they brought her here. Walking down the hall to the front door revealed how large the house was. And how wrecked. Holes in the walls and more garbage scattered here and there. The house was completely unkempt.

The front door sat open, light coming in from the headlights of an SUV.

"How did you find me?" she asked.

"I was informed AOV gang members had jumped those two FBI agents you were with. I spotted one checking out a warehouse earlier today and followed him here. I waited until most of them were gone, and here we are."

They stepped outside the front door cautiously, the man going first. He had his gun out, pointed at the ground.

"I didn't get your name," Sarah whispered.

"Just call me Bruce."

She nodded, leaning on the wall for support.

"All clear," he said. "Let's go."

He walked out onto the porch and down the steps. Sarah followed.

Two AOV men were lying on the fresh snow. They appeared to be sleeping peacefully.

"What did you do to them?"

"Chloroform."

"Chloroform? Where would you get that?"

"You'd be surprised what the police department has access to."

He walked her to the passenger side and opened the door for her. Once she was inside and secure, he walked around to his side and got in.

He started backing down a long driveway. It looked like the AOV gang had broken into a farmhouse lost to bankruptcy or something and used it as a base for a while.

"Where are we going now?"

"Lyson wants to see you."

Something bothered her. Her instinct told her to be careful here.

"Where's your backup?" she asked.

"You've heard of surgical insurgence?"

"I can guess what it means."

"That's what this was. More men would've complicated things."

"Those AOV men back there in the snow weren't sleeping off chloroform, were they?"

He stopped backing up and spun the vehicle around. The headlights shined on a snow-covered road.

"I used chloroform. They were sleeping. The only difference is they will never wake up. I might have used too much." The dash's glow offered enough light to reveal a sinister smile. He looked sideways at her. "Don't worry, Sarah. I'll get you safely to Lyson. You have my word."

She turned in her seat and looked in the back. Two large metal cases took up most of the back seat.

"What's in those?"

"Lyson searched the warehouse where I saw the AOV member earlier today. When he did this search a few days back, he removed a quantity of C-4."

"And what's it doing here?"

"After I drop you off, I'm taking it to be disposed of."

They wouldn't transport it this way.

Her cousin Russell had called the house to warn her. And now bombs were in the back seat. Lyson would've had the bomb squad dispose of them. He wouldn't have them riding around in an SUV, especially not in the vehicle of the man dispatched to free her.

She was free from the street gang but with someone called Bruce.

Something about Bruce told her he wasn't on her side.

She opened the glove box looking for a weapon. It was empty.

"What are you doing?" he asked.

"Who are you really? Where are we going?"

"I'm taking you to Lyson." He smiled.

She shut the glove box. The words Range Rover were printed on the little door.

She sat back and waited to see what was coming. Vivian gave her the address with tonight's date and time on it. This man was driving her to Lyson or the warehouse with the explosives in the back.

Could he be the man Lyson was hunting? Too many things didn't make sense. What was waiting for her at the warehouse on Keele Street?

She only hoped they didn't get into a car accident on the way there.

Then none of her questions would get answered, and Russell would've been correct again.

Sarah would be dead.

Chapter 31

DEATH STEPPED INTO THE room where the party was in full swing. Juan was drunk, his girlfriend had already passed out on the couch. He had arranged to borrow the clubhouse of a friendly gang that owed him a favor. The MS-13 was a seriously violent gang also. They were larger and better connected than AOV. Recently, Death had arranged a couple of drug mules for them as they were connected to large cartels south of the border. Along with payment, he had asked for the use of the clubhouse for the evening.

When asked why he told his contact what he needed to do, they loved the idea.

The time had come to finish up here and head over to the prearranged carpool lot where he was to meet the two men who were guarding Sarah. They were to bring her to him so he could take her downtown for her own violent death. He had a plan worked out, and everything was already in place.

Juan stumbled on his feet, his thigh still wrapped in bandages. After correcting himself with a wooden crutch under his right arm, he hobbled the few feet to the wall, where he leaned on it for support.

"Where's that bitch, Sarah?" Juan asked. "Aren't we all going to take a turn on her? She dies tonight, right?"

"Oh yes, Sarah dies tonight."

"That bitch shot me!"

"We know. But there's something else we have to deal with first."

Death had ordered his driver to refrain from having more than one alcoholic beverage. Once they were done here, he was to go with him to meet the two men he left behind with Sarah.

What she didn't know was that the warehouse wasn't high enough. The roof of the Royal Oak Hotel in downtown Toronto was much better. The splat would be quite a sight. He smiled to himself as he stared at Juan, who tried to stay upright.

The music blared from the speakers. He had an hour to get to the prearranged spot to pick Sarah up.

It was time to teach Juan what his disloyalty had bought him.

Without pause, Death stepped forward, balled his fist, pulled back, and before Juan saw him coming, drove his knuckles into Juan's cheek hard enough to snap his head back.

Juan crumpled to the floor and writhed back and forth, holding his cheek.

"Wha'ya do that for?" Juan mumbled.

The music died. Everyone knew what was coming, but

only five men Death had picked previously were to be involved.

Two of them lifted him up as he shouted for answers and carried him into one of the back rooms. The room where the plastic sheet had already been set up.

The other three grabbed Juan's unconscious girlfriend.

"Hook him up," Death ordered.

Chains hung from the ceiling. Juan resisted, but in his drunken state, he was no match for the strength of Death's strongest men. When they were done, Juan was suspended in the air, his arms stretched out, his legs opened as well, forming a human X. He hung two feet off the plastic-covered floor.

"Bring the buckets over," Death ordered. "I want to catch as much blood as we can."

Juan wept. "Why are you doing this, man?" he asked. "Please, what did I do?"

"You turned on us."

"No, I never. You know I would never do that. I didn't say shit when they had me in that cell."

"When your whore was doing her initiation, she wanted it to stop."

"That's on her. Do it again, then. Kill her if you have to."

Death moved in close. He pulled a long blade out of a sheath attached to his belt. He placed the tip to Juan's face and pushed it against his skin. "You helped stop her initiation. You got in the way. That's disloyal to the rite and to AOV members everywhere. Then you ran after her."

Juan leaned away from the knife, keeping his eyes on Death. "I was just helping a member—"

"She wasn't a member yet!" Death roared and slashed

downward.

The knife cut easily from the bottom of Juan's cheek to under his jaw. He wailed and thrashed in the chains as blood ran down his face.

"Cut his clothes off," Death ordered. Juan's girlfriend stirred at the sound of Juan's scream. "Make sure she doesn't wake yet. If she does, knock her out."

Juan breathed in and out heavily, his face red. Two men stepped up with knives in their hands and slashed at Juan's jeans. As they cut and yanked his clothes from his body, they paid no attention to the bandages on his thigh.

Hanging naked before them, Juan pleaded again. "Please, let me make it right. I'll fix it. Tell me what to do."

"We are fixing it. You're playing your part already. Don't irritate me, or I'll cut your eyes out first and not last."

Death turned to his men, who stood waiting on the side. "Have you got the blow torch?"

"Yes."

"Bring it here. Fire it up. As I cut, seal the wound with the flame. I want him alive as long as we can."

Juan screamed.

"The rest of you," Death gestured at the other men who had been drinking at the party. "Take his girlfriend and have your fun until she's dead. Do not bring her back in here breathing. Now go."

One of them walked over and dragged her out of the room by her arm.

The blow torch started.

Death approached Juan and set the blade between Juan's legs.

"When someone is disloyal to AOV, he is killed in the

most vile way possible. Enjoy your punishment."

He pulled Juan's scrotum down as far as possible and then cut along the base with the blade.

"Burn him," he shouted over Juan's screams.

Juan's girlfriend woke up in the other room. Her screams matched Juan's. Then Juan threw up and passed out with the pain.

"Wake him up!" he shouted.

Then Death smiled.

Chapter 32

THE DASH CLOCK SAID they had twenty minutes left of leap day. Sarah was still getting familiar with the streets of Toronto, but by following street signs, she guessed they were only a few blocks from the warehouse address Vivian had given her.

"Where's Lyson meeting me?" she asked.

"He requested a meet in a warehouse on Keele Street."

"Why not at the police station?"

"While you were away, Lyson received another letter from the sick fuck who has been killing women every four years."

"What did it say?"

"That he wanted to meet you and Lyson at the warehouse alone, or he wouldn't show up. Lyson assumes that means he would disappear forever."

"So we're going to meet this killer?" Sarah asked.

Bruce nodded. He slowed the vehicle and turned a corner. It was a dark street without even one parked car. They eased along until Bruce turned into the empty parking lot of a deserted warehouse.

"This is it," Bruce said. He pointed at the dash clock. "Lyson should be here any minute. You ready?"

"I have no idea what I'm supposed to be ready for, so yeah, I guess I am."

She couldn't allow him to detonate the bombs in the back seat, or she would die, as would Lyson and anyone else he brought with him.

The problem was she had no idea how the bombs were to be detonated.

"How long have you worked with the police department?" she asked.

"Better part of thirty years."

"Wow, long time."

"As the medical examiner," he added.

"A medical examiner who invades an Angels of Violence clubhouse?"

He turned his head slowly to look at her. "You were at the crisis center. Why would you taunt your boyfriend to hurt you? You sound like a nice girl. Look what happened to you because of your mouth. When will women ever learn?"

His outburst stunned her for a moment. "What are you talking about?"

"This is the ultimate reset. I make things right for those that do wrong. I make two women pay every four years for the sins of their kind—"

Sarah lunged across the seat, her fists already balled up, aiming for his face and throat. She barely got two hits in before her door was yanked open from the outside.

Someone grabbed her ankles and pulled hard.

She was pulled off the driver, slid along the seat, and headed for the open door. She couldn't find anything to grab onto fast enough, so she twisted at the last second so her face wouldn't smack into the ground when she exited the vehicle.

Her twist spun her out of the person's grip, but she still landed hard on the snow-packed parking lot.

A car door slammed as Bruce got out on the other side.

A moment later, he stood above her, a gun trained on her face.

"Sarah, I'd like you to meet my sister. You remember Jennifer from the crisis center, don't you?"

"Get her up and bring her inside," Jennifer said. "You can't stay out front where the cops could pick us off. I'll stay with the Range Rover and ensure we're set to go."

Bruce grabbed Sarah's wrist right on the spot where the manacles had been chained to her for the better part of the last week. She clenched her teeth and tried not to make any sounds.

She got to her feet, spun around, and made to jab him in the throat with her thumb, but instead had the tip of his gun hit her in the mouth, the steel rubbing her teeth and gums.

"Don't be stupid, Sarah. This is a suicide mission. You think I need you anymore? You're here. I'm here. Now we wait for Lyson to show. Once he's here, Jennifer will blow all the evidence up. She has the detonator. Don't be stupid, or she'll blow us up early. You wouldn't want that, now would you?"

He pushed so hard with the weapon that she had to crank her neck back or start eating the gun.

He took her silence as an answer.

"Good. Now turn around and be a good girl for once. Walk ahead of me at least three feet. Do anything else and die for your efforts."

Chapter 33

DEATH WASHED THE BLOOD off his hands and forearms in the bathroom sink. Juan had screamed until he passed out again and again, but the smelling salts worked wonderfully to bring him around each time.

Death made sure the display of violence while executing Juan was extreme and completely over the top. No more would he allow active members to think they could ever do anything close to what Juan had done. Juan had been the example, and Death felt satisfied with how things went.

He toweled dry and stepped from the bathroom. At the end of the hall, in the other room, his men were cleaning up the leftover body parts of Juan's girlfriend. In an hour, all evidence of them ever having been in this clubhouse would disappear in the barrel of acid in the garage. Juan and his girlfriend would never be found, and life would motor on for Death and his followers.

There were drugs to sell, guns to move, and whores to whore out. He had an important meeting with a known associate of a cartel coming up in two weeks. If things went well, AOV's Toronto chapter would rock and roll. They would be on the map for good, and the authorities would approach with care when dealing with them in the future.

He walked the length of the clubhouse and stepped out into the cold night. The car idled, waiting for him, his driver warm inside.

With one last look over his shoulder, Death walked down the shoveled path and out the large gate to the waiting vehicle.

Once inside, his driver started off right away.

"Have you heard from the house?" Death asked. "Are they on their way with Sarah?"

Enrico shook his head. "Nothing."

"They were supposed to call."

The driver's phone was on the dash. Death grabbed it and dialed the men at the house. When there was no answer, he dropped the phone on the seat beside him.

"Hit the gas. Get me to the carpool lot. They should be answering their phone. Something's not right."

"They'll be there, they'll be there."

Death looked sideways at the driver. "Why are you so sure, ese?"

"Because they know what you had planned for Juan. No way they gonna fuck this up."

He leaned back in his seat and watched the scenery go by, thinking about Sarah Roberts. Too bad a girl like that wasn't with him, running the Toronto chapter of AOV. She had shot Juan. She had brass balls, and he could really use that in a woman.

But he could never keep her. No, tonight she flew from the top of the downtown hotel. Tonight Sarah was going to find out what it was like to grow wings before she hit the ground.

It's that sudden stop at the end that's a bitch.

Chapter 34

"Remember, you're lucky you're even on this ride-along," Lyson whispered. "I shouldn't have allowed it knowing how close you and Sarah are."

"They have Sarah. Your medical examiner has a gun on her. I say we go after them."

Lyson eased back around the edge of the building that concealed them. "Aaron, there won't be any cowboy stuff. We don't operate that way. I have fifty officers, half of them the Emergency Task Force, waiting five blocks away for my call. They will take the medical examiner out of that building. Don't worry. We've got him now."

Aaron stepped away from Lyson. He shook his head. "You're wrong. That man has Sarah—"

"Lower your voice," Lyson snapped, spittle coming from his mouth.

"You're supposed to meet him with Sarah. We haven't

seen her for almost a week, and he shows up with her. And you're just going to send in reinforcements?" Aaron stepped farther away. "That man has no issue with killing women. Consider that Sarah is his hostage. How do you even know if Sarah still has her tongue? What if that monster tore hers out, too?" Aaron turned and watched the threesome across the street. The woman did something in the back of the Range Rover. "You think she lives when your men storm the building? We have to do something."

"Stand down," Lyson said.

His tone was low and menacing. Aaron looked over his shoulder at him.

Lyson had his hand on the butt of his gun. "We do this the official way. This is police business. No vigilante shit tonight. I will not have my retirement ruined by this."

Aaron straightened up and moved closer to Lyson. "You're right," he whispered. "It has to be done the right way, the official way. Call in the backup then."

Lyson lowered his hand and reached for the radio.

Aaron moved fast, stepping in and snapping Lyson's weapon from his holster. Lyson's gun was in Aaron's belt line before Lyson could protest.

"What the hell was that? Give me back my sidearm."

"Arrest me tomorrow. I'm going after Sarah."

"You can't," Lyson snapped and stepped forward.

Aaron eased in before Lyson could react. He spun Lyson around and wrapped his arms gently around Lyson's neck, adding just enough pressure to get Lyson asleep in less than a minute. Then he lowered him to the ground, knowing he wouldn't freeze or even get frostbite before Aaron would be back.

At the edge of the building, he looked across the street. The woman was alone now, still doing something in the back of the Rover.

Sarah and the male were gone.

He stepped out into the open, pulled Lyson's gun from his belt, and started across the parking lot, heading straight at the woman. Every minute he couldn't see Sarah was another moment he feared the worst.

The street had been cleared of snow, so his footfalls were silent. Snow and ice covered the parking lot of the abandoned warehouse. As soon as he stepped onto it, the woman would be able to hear him.

Any second, she could turn around and see him in the wide open, a gun in his hand.

He put the gun in the back of his pants, ruffled up his hair, and stepped onto the ice. He got four steps before the woman leaned out of the back of the vehicle and turned around. In the limited glow from the streetlights, it looked like she held a TV remote in her hand.

"Stop right there," she ordered.

He took one more step and then stopped. They stood ten feet apart. He estimated he could make her in two large steps, then one jump.

"Who are you?" she asked. "You don't look like police."

"Police?" Aaron asked, appearing fearful at the sound of the word. "Why police? I wanted to bum a cigarette off you. I'm walking home after a long shift."

The woman looked both ways up the road. Her eyes lingered a moment on Keele Street.

"You're walking home where? This is an industrial area."

"Just got off work. I live on the other side of that bridge."

He pointed, then waited.

She turned away to look at the train bridge.

He lunged. One step, two steps, then he jumped, his right foot aimed at the thing in the woman's hand.

She caught his movement and tried to duck out of the way.

But he had already zeroed in on the TV remote, hitting it from her hand perfectly. It flew away, landing in a small pile of fresh snow about fifteen feet from them.

By the time he landed and turned to deal with her, she turned to run.

He grabbed her right arm and spun her around. She pivoted on her feet and bent over from the pressure he applied on her arm. Aaron flicked her wrist up backward, now controlling her every movement.

She looked up at him sideways, her face strained.

Their eyes met briefly. He hated to hit women, but this one hurt Sarah, and he needed her to be quiet while he entered the warehouse.

She opened her mouth to scream, and he dropped a knee into her temple so fast that her head snapped sideways on her neck, and her body dropped.

He lifted her unconscious body over his shoulder and walked across to Lyson's car as fast as he could go with her weight.

At the car, he set her in the back seat and then went over to Lyson. He dragged him to the car, lifted him into the driver's seat, and then yanked the cuffs off his belt. He used the cuffs to secure the woman in the back seat of the car.

If she woke before Aaron got back or before Lyson woke, she wouldn't be going anywhere or doing any more damage.

Then he straightened up and looked at the warehouse across the street.

"Here I come, Sarah. Here I come."

He touched the gun at the back of his pants to ensure it was still there.

Then he ran.

Chapter 35

"Where are we going, asshole?" Sarah asked.

"Name-calling won't save you."

"No, but it makes me feel better."

"The side door. It's unlocked."

"Why are you doing this?" Sarah asked. "Seriously, is there a rational answer to that question in your irrational world?"

"Because it's over."

"No, I mean, why do it in the first place? Those girls didn't know you or hurt you. Or did they?"

"I have been given a raw deal when it comes to women. Every time I have had to deal with them, I've had to pay a price. I hate how men get the worst out of the arrangement."

"That's not always the case. Women get screwed over, too. But that's not reason enough to hurt and kill people. Come on, surely you can see that?"

"Yeah, sure, but it never balances out. Men always end up worse off. Just check divorce stats and see that men are left with nothing but payments while the ex-wife lives in their matrimonial home, driving their kids to practices in their car. I'm adjusting the balance bit by bit. Resetting things. Making them right. I have never cared if it's right for someone else. I know it's right for me."

They reached the side door of the warehouse. He pushed it open without resistance.

"Get inside."

She did what she was told. Red exit signs and emergency lighting lit the vast interior in the dark. When she looked back, Bruce stood close behind her.

"So what's this then? A suicide mission?"

"Not really. I'm calling this the ultimate reset."

"Why's that?"

"With my sister and me dead, it will right the wrongs we've committed. It's the only way."

"I'm not following your logic. A minute ago, you sounded like you were doing the right thing, but now you're going to die because of the wrongs you've committed. Sounds crazy to me."

He lunged forward and pushed her shoulder, making her step back.

"Don't call it crazy. I'm a medical examiner. I deal with dead bodies all the time. I'm not crazy. Everything I've ever done has been thought out and planned for a long time. This is my swan song. This is the end." His voice created an echo in the building. "They didn't even know about me until I sent them a letter telling them what I had done and where the bodies were. Fucking cops had no clue."

"So let's kill a few of them," she said, the anger coming through in her voice.

"Shut up and move to that corner."

He directed her toward the front of the building. She didn't have any weapons on her, but even in the darkness of the warehouse, there was just enough light to see the glint off the barrel of his weapon, so she started walking.

At the scrape of metal on metal, she jumped into the defensive position Aaron had taught her. Someone was entering through the side door they had just walked through.

She turned around, but Bruce wasn't behind her anymore.

Then another man stepped into the light from the exit sign over the side door.

Chapter 36

DEATH GOT OUT OF the car and checked each and every vehicle at the carpool lot. None of them held his two men and Sarah.

Something had gone wrong.

"People are going to die over this," he said as he slammed a fist into the open palm of his other hand.

He jumped back in the car and verified the time.

"They're more than late. They knew where to come. Something happened."

"What do you want me to do?" Enrico asked. "Drive to the house?"

"Let me think."

Death tapped his leg, stared out the front window, and wondered how it could all go wrong. Two men. One woman. One chained-up woman. Maybe he underestimated her. She looked strong, tough. Talked that way, too. Were two men enough to guard someone like her?

"Shit. Take me to the warehouse on Keele Street."

"Why there?"

"Drive!" Death shouted.

After they were underway, he added, "It's possible, unlikely, but possible, that our guys thought we were meeting there. I had said the warehouse for Sarah's benefit. But the roof wasn't high enough."

"Maybe that's it," Enrico agreed.

"Or Sarah did something to escape. If so, she would come to the warehouse looking for me because I told her I would be there. She strikes me as that kind of woman."

Five minutes later, Death told him to pull over on the south side of the train bridge.

"Why here? We gotta cross the bridge and take the first right."

"No. I'm going in the back way. If someone's there, I'll surprise them. You stay here."

"Here?"

Death looked at him. "Are you fucking deaf? Stay here. When I whistle, drive around to the front, and pick me up. Keep your car window down and listen for my whistle."

Enrico nodded. "Whatever you say."

Death got out, checked the knife on his hip, and started walking. The car turned off behind him.

"Someone's gonna pay for this fuck up," Death said to himself. "Someone's gonna pay, big time."

Death started running.

Chapter 37

AARON STEVENS STOOD JUST inside the warehouse door, his empty hands flared out to his side.

"Sarah?" he called. "You okay?"

"Good to see you, too. Where have you been? Could've used you over the past few days."

"Sorry, babe. Been busy. Hunting this asshole." Aaron nodded at Bruce. "Come on, Martin. Give it up."

"Martin?" Sarah asked. She looked at him. "Not Bruce?"

"Not Bruce," Martin said. "Now shut up and keep moving toward the front of the warehouse. We've got over half the building to cover." He waved his gun toward the front.

Then he casually turned the gun toward Aaron, raised it, and fired, the sound deafening in the empty warehouse.

Aaron ducked out of reflex and dropped to the ground. He did it so fast that it almost looked like gravity had stopped working under him. Then he rolled up against the wall and was lost from sight.

"What? No warning?" Aaron shouted. "Fuck!"

Sarah edged backward slowly, trying for a pillar about eight feet away. She had to get something between her and Martin.

The gun swung back to her. "Don't make me shoot you, too."

She stopped.

Aaron stayed hidden.

"You hit, Aaron?" Sarah asked.

"No, but that was close."

"What happened to Jennifer?" Martin asked over his shoulder.

"That bitch at the Range Rover?"

"She's not a bitch. She spends her life helping women do the right thing. She chose an honorable profession. What happened to her?"

"She's in police custody. Banged up, but in custody."

"Liar. Lyson wouldn't show up with his friends. He knew the deal, and it was too serious to fuck around with."

"I'm his friend," Aaron's voice echoed throughout the warehouse. "I'm here. So you're wrong."

"How come Lyson isn't here?"

"He sleeping."

"What's to stop me from pushing the detonator button? It looks like my work is done here."

Aaron stayed silent. Sweat trickled down Sarah's forehead even though it was cold in the warehouse.

"You're bluffing," she said. "You don't have a detonator. Your sister had it."

"You think I would come this far and not be prepared?"

"Prepared?" Sarah said in his tone. "I'm sick of people like you. If you had a problem with the way things were, fix it. People like you are *de*structive, not *con*structive. You don't fix things by killing people. What is wrong with you?" She thought about what she had just said. "Wait, I take that back. Unless they're people like you."

He aimed the gun at her face. "You see," he said. "That's the shit I have to take from women. Why can't you just shut up? I would've killed you last."

There was movement behind him. She guessed Aaron was creeping closer, remaining silent. In mere seconds he would be behind Martin.

"But you *are* an asshole," she continued, keeping his attention riveted on her. She tried to study his hand in the dim light to catch the movement of his finger to see if it depressed the trigger. "A dirty piece of shit. How about you drop the gun and come and fight me? You're only as tough as your weapon. Fucking child, that's what you are—"

Aaron was in the air, his foot aimed high.

The gun went first, kicked so hard that Martin's wrist snapped before the gun hit the floor. Aaron's other foot landed perfectly on the side of Martin's head, knocking him into the air sideways. Then they were both sprawled out on the floor of the warehouse.

Sarah ran to Aaron and reached for the gun on the way, but he was already getting up.

Martin's good hand disappeared inside his jacket.

Aaron dove for him. Sarah turned and kicked at Martin's arm, hoping that he didn't have a detonator.

At the second the three bodies converged, a large

explosion imploded the warehouse's front wall, tossing huge chunks of metal and concrete toward them. The shock wave shoved them along the floor at least a dozen feet.

Her hearing temporarily gone, and the building suddenly cast in darkness as all the lights went out, Sarah covered her head and waited for the debris to stop falling.

The weight of a body had landed on her.

She closed her eyes and screamed Aaron's name, hoping he was okay.

Chapter 38

DEATH DESCENDED TO THE train tracks, carefully ran over them in the dark, and climbed up the other side. When he reached the top of the embankment on the warehouse side, an explosion knocked him back. He staggered on his feet.

"What the fuck was that?"

He wondered if it had anything to do with him. Could Sarah have had a plan all this time?

Death ran across the field, arms pumping hard as he went, the knife on his belt snapping into his thigh with every step. Anyone close to the building when the explosion happened would've been knocked off their feet, so he had no fear of running into anyone.

Sirens screamed from a few blocks away. When he got to the warehouse, he wouldn't have much time. If Sarah were here and still alive, he would do everything he could to take her with him.

He stopped running thirty meters short of the ruined warehouse wall and whistled. Enrico flashed the car lights and started over the bridge.

Death continued running toward the warehouse. He looked along the side wall that was somewhat still intact near the back. Halfway up, it crumpled in, and near the front was completely gone. What was left of a vehicle burned in the parking lot out front, casting an eerie light on the premises as the street lights were all out in front of the warehouse.

Enrico eased into the warehouse parking lot slowly, his lights off.

Sirens were only blocks away.

Death scanned the building for a way in. He ran the length of the wall and climbed in over the rubble that had collected where a side door used to be.

"Anyone still alive in here?" Death asked.

"Over here," a man shouted back. "Help me. Sarah's trapped."

"On my way," Death said.

He pulled his knife out and started toward the voice.

Chapter 39

SARAH CUPPED HER HANDS in front of her face to breathe. The body on her wasn't moving, but the weight of that body was so much that she couldn't move under it.

Her hearing returned slowly, sounds coming as if through a tunnel. She took two deep breaths and pushed up and to the side.

Nothing moved.

Shit.

She tried again. Aaron's voice broke through from far away, telling her to remain still.

Hearing him and realizing that he wasn't the lifeless body on her was a great relief. She let the air out of her lungs and focused on her breathing. The warehouse air was gritty with dust. There was a rank smell about it, and she covered her nose again before she breathed in.

The weight on her back adjusted, then settled again.

Aaron's voice grew louder as her hearing returned.

"Anyone still alive in here?" a man asked.

That's not Aaron's voice, but I recognize it.

"Over here," Aaron shouted. "Help me. Sarah's trapped."

"On my way," the other voice responded.

Her stomach stirred at the sound of that voice. The explosion had knocked her down. She had slid on the floor and banged her head. Things weren't coming together yet.

The weight adjusted again.

"Sarah, stay still," Aaron said. "There's a small chunk of concrete leaning on Martin's back. Once we pry it off, we'll get him off you." He was close, but she couldn't see him. She breathed in and out through her hands.

"Looks like this chunk snapped his back," Aaron said. "Okay, Sarah, we've got a metal bar. We'll try to pry the concrete off Martin's body. Hold tight."

Her hearing was good enough to make out the sounds of grunting as two men worked the bar. Emergency sirens were close now.

Then the weight was gone. Blood flowed freely to her legs. She flexed her ankles and hands and turned over as Martin's dead body rolled off her.

"Thanks, guys," she said as Aaron took her hand and helped her slowly to a sitting position.

Then the other voice registered.

"Death ..." she muttered.

"What?" Aaron asked.

Headlights turned on at the front of the building, shining through the large hole the explosion made. Silhouetted in their glow, a man stood behind Aaron.

The man held a metal bar, but he was holding it like a

baseball bat.

"Aaron. Look out!"

Death swung. Aaron ducked.

But not fast enough.

The bar hit Aaron above the ear. He crumpled to the floor like jelly, as if his body had no bones.

"Come on, bitch. We're going to finish this."

The knife in Death's hand glinted in the light. He grabbed her forearm and yanked her to her feet. He leaned back and did something to Aaron, but she couldn't see what. She resisted his grip to pull him away from Aaron, but with his incredible strength, he brought her in close and jammed the blade against the underside of her jaw.

"Pull away again, and I'll bleed you like a pig. Don't fuck with Death."

A horn blared outside. Red lights strobed through the night, coming closer.

Death ran, yanking Sarah behind him, her dazed mind wondering how she would cope if Aaron were just killed in front of her.

At an opening in the wall, Death hopped out and pulled her out behind him. She stayed on her feet but almost tripped when he wrapped an arm around her neck.

"Stay close. Trying to run or shout for help will only get you killed. You saw what we did to those FBI guys. Killing cops don't bother me." He pointed. "That car. Go."

Emergency vehicles were lined up a block away. She figured the fire trucks were staying back until the bomb squad got here to make sure there was no more danger. Two police cars screamed up Keele Street on the other side of the snowy field.

The Range Rover she arrived in was gone. In its place, a black hole was cut in the snow. Across the street, an unmarked cruiser sat parked by an office building, its lights out. It looked like its windows were all broken in from the explosion.

When they reached the waiting vehicle, Death shoved her into the back seat. He jumped in behind her.

"Go," he shouted to the driver, who spun the car around and drove away from Keele Street, the lights off.

It's all my fault, she thought.

She had allowed herself to get close to Aaron. He had come for her and paid the ultimate price.

She would go with Death. Killing him in the back seat of his car wouldn't be good enough. She stared at the side of his head. No, she would kill him in the most violent way possible.

If it was the last thing she did.

Chapter 40

RUSSELL ANDERSON HAD SPENT a considerable amount of money to check into the hotel two days ago. He had told them he was here on business, in Toronto, from the States as a sanitation advisor. At least, that's what Penny had told him to do. That explained the two metal garbage cans in his room, the kind with metal lids and handles. Why the ruse was beyond him, but since Penny had died years ago at the hand of a madwoman, she had whispered prophecies into Russell's consciousness, and he listened.

When he met his cousin, Sarah Roberts, those messages saved both their lives in Vegas.

Tonight he guessed the messages were only for Sarah.

Penny had instructed him to take two lids off the metal cans and go to the twenty-eighth floor tonight after midnight. He was to wait until an employee of the hotel showed up to open the door to the roof. Knock him out and gain access to the roof.

Sarah was in danger, and a man was coming to the roof to do her harm. Russell was supposed to stop that from happening.

Then he would get to see his dead daughter.

At least that's as much as he got from Penny. He had waited a long time to get to this day. The search for his father in Vegas had turned out favorably, but now that Russell had been in Toronto for the last five months, he hadn't spent a lot of time with him.

It had been a month since their last call.

All he had was Penny. All he wanted was to hold his daughter again.

She'd promised him all that.

He got up from the bed, walked over to the garbage cans, and picked up the two lids.

Then he checked himself in the mirror. Bags had formed under his eyes. Weariness creased the lines on his face, and depression had become him. If only things had worked out with Penny's mother, life would've gone another way.

But it hadn't, and now he had a chance to help a family member.

He looked away from his reflection and left the hotel room. At this late hour, the corridor was empty. He headed for the stairs.

At the highest level near the roof access, he backed into a recess in the wall beside a large box that contained a fire extinguisher and waited.

It wouldn't be long now.

Then he would do what was required of him.

Only then would Penny come back to him.

He couldn't live without her anymore.
He wept while he waited.

Chapter 41

AARON WOKE UP AND jumped to his feet. His head swam, and he clutched it where the pain resonated.

"What the …"

The building around him shook in his vision, then slowly calmed and became still. His stomach rolled around. He needed to rest. Maybe he had a concussion.

Sarah.

He snapped his head up. The room swam again.

Gotta help Sarah.

He started for the door, putting everything together as he went. The explosion. The TV remote in the woman's hand outside had been a detonator. Martin had had one too.

But now Martin was dead.

Aaron jumped outside. The sirens had stopped, emergency vehicle lights filled the night. Men in uniform ran toward him. It was dark enough beside the building that he couldn't tell if they were police or paramedics.

"Hands up!" the man closest to him shouted.

Aaron leaned against the side of the building and raised his hands.

"You guys got Sarah?" he asked.

"That's Aaron Stevens," a familiar voice said.

Detective Alan Lyson.

Aaron lowered his hands.

"Look what you've done," Lyson shouted.

"What are you talking about?" Aaron knew he'd fucked up. But he had tried, and if it weren't for that other guy, Sarah would be fine right now. He had succeeded—sort of. "I stopped the woman and put her in your cruiser. I even handcuffed her for you."

"You attacked a police officer when things weren't going your way. Then you dealt with the situation your way, and look what happened. This building is destroyed, and I don't see Sarah with you. Or the medical examiner."

"The medical examiner is dead. When he hit the detonator, flying concrete cut him down."

"Where's Sarah?" Lyson asked.

Aaron wiped at the blood that had trickled down his face. "I thought you guys had her." Men ran past them and into the building, flashlights in hand. "She came out with a guy a few minutes ago," Aaron added. "The same guy who hit me."

"What guy?" Lyson asked, veins popping on his forehead and neck. He turned to a man on his right. "Your guys were the first responders. Did anyone leave this building?"

"We didn't see a soul. There was a car, but it was near the end of the street going the other way when we saw it."

"There was a car," Lyson repeated. He looked back at

Aaron. "Well then. That about wraps this case up. The serial killer is dead. His sister is under arrest, and Sarah Roberts is in a car going who knows where."

"We have to do something," Aaron said as he pushed off the wall.

"Where's my gun?" Lyson asked.

Aaron reached around and felt nothing in his belt line. "Shit."

Lyson leaned in close to Aaron. "I'm supposed to retire next month. And now my police issue sidearm has been stolen. If it's used to commit a crime …" He left it unfinished.

"We have to do something—"

"*We* aren't going to do anything. Aaron Stevens, you're under arrest."

"What? You can't do that," Aaron shouted.

"Take him away and read him his rights. Now!"

Chapter 42

Sarah sat squished up against the door, Death's hips pushing into hers. He gripped his knife with the blade parallel to his forearm, the tip of the blade resting against her crotch. When the car hit bumps, the tip snagged her jeans.

"Is that really necessary?" she asked.

"Try anything, and you get fucked with a knife."

"Thanks for that image. Where are we going?"

"How did you know all that shit was going to happen at the warehouse?" Death asked. "Is that why you wanted me to use it? So some of my crew would be killed?"

"I had no idea *what* was going to happen."

"But you knew something."

"Do you realize the shit storm coming after you?" Sarah asked.

"What happened to the men I left behind with you?" Death asked, the knife edging closer, pushing slightly on the denim near her crotch. "How is it you are not chained to a wall? Those men would die before they betrayed me."

"They are dead."

Death moaned and ground his teeth together. Sarah waited for her move. The driver slowed for a right turn.

Death moved in his seat beside her. His hip came away from hers as the knife slipped away slightly.

Sarah drove her right hand down, using her open palm in a tiger fist, and smashed into Death's knife hand so hard the knife dislodged from his grip, tumbling to the floor mat.

He was already reaching for her hair, but she brought her arm up and drove her elbow toward his face.

His speed surprised her as his face was no longer there. In that second pause, a sharp pain coursed through her ribs. Then another.

She shouted as the car turned the corner, her weight pushed into the car door.

Death shouted with her, a screeching wail.

Somehow he had pulled away far enough to use his other hand and punch her twice in the side of the ribs. Each breath became a labor of pain. He had to have cracked a rib for sure. Maybe two.

But she had to fight through the pain because she was sure his wrist was either sprained or broken. Getting out of this car was the only way to survive.

She shut her mouth, gritted her teeth, and turned to him, ready to go for his eyes.

But Death held a gun now. Where it came from so fast, she had no idea. Instinctively, she backed away from the weapon until her head touched the window behind her.

"You jammed my wrist up," Death screamed. "That

fucking hurts. It might be broken."

"You broke my ribs—"

"Shut up." Death shouted so loud the driver turned around in his seat. "Drive the car. Get us there. I want to watch this bitch fly. Then I'll take a photo of the bloody corpse. If we had more time, I would fuck your corpse, but you're not worth it."

He spit at her, his phlegm landing on her shoulder. "I don't care how this ends," Death said. "But it ends tonight. No one attacks the Angels of Violence and lives." He pushed the gun against her chin. "You've fucked up my plan, big time."

"Everyone has a plan until I break one of their bones," she said. "Things always change after that."

She glimpsed the weapon's safety was still on, and he only had the use of one hand.

He followed her glimpse to the safety and then body-checked her into the door. While using his weight to hold her still, her ribs screaming at the pain, he flicked the safety to the off position.

Then the pressure was gone. He sat on the other side of the back seat and held the gun with his good hand, resting it on the back of the front seat.

"Get us there fast," he yelled at the driver. "Or I will shoot this bitch in the face."

"We're almost there," the driver said.

"Drive faster!" Death shouted.

Chapter 43

Russell waited. He had stopped crying and began to meditate. Thoughts of his daughter ran through his mind. How he yearned to be with her again. His life had gone from one disaster to another. He had spent the few years since her death losing everything he owned in a bid to locate the family denied to him by a mother who lied about his existence.

Even Sarah didn't know they were cousins until six months ago. When Sarah had called her mother and asked, the truth was denied again.

His credit cards were maxed out, and his line of credit on his bank account covered the hotel, but collections letters were coming to his apartment in Vegas.

With no job, no desire to get one, and nothing to live for, family had been his last remaining straw to grasp.

Sarah lived a life too dangerous for him. He didn't like

getting involved. He didn't want to hurt anyone. There was enough pain in the world, and he didn't want to add to it.

But if family was in trouble and he could do something about it, he had to. Penny was family, and no one helped her.

Knowing he could see Penny when this was all over was all he needed. Deep in his soul, he knew what that meant. There was really only one way to see Penny.

The cruel world had left him with no other option.

A door banged down the hallway. A moment later, footsteps came toward him.

Then a man dressed in the hotel uniform stepped through the door in front of him and pulled keys out. He flipped through the key ring that held at least twenty keys, found the one he was searching for, and inserted it into the door.

Wind from the roof rushed through, opening the door faster than the man had intended. When it banged against the wall, he glimpsed Russell hiding in the corner.

"Hey, what you doing here?"

Russell got up, holding one of the garbage can lids like a shield.

"I'm sorry." He pulled out his room key to calm the guy down. "I got lost. Don't know my way around. My mom always said I shouldn't wander."

He stepped closer, lowering the shield to his side.

"Well, you have to go back to your room."

"Yes, sir, right away, sir."

Russell turned to go through the door that led into the hotel, stopped, and slammed it shut.

"Hey, what are you—"

His words were cut off as the garbage can lid connected with his jaw. The blow had the desired effect, knocking the employee down and out.

Penny had told Russell that the man was helping Death. The employee on the floor understood that opening the door to the roof for Death was supposed to get him a free pass to come to a street gang's clubhouse as payment.

The man on the floor didn't have a future. Hitting him hard enough to knock him out and possibly break his jaw might just give him the future that would have been denied him had he joined a street gang.

Russell set the shield down and grabbed the man's arms. He dragged him out onto the roof and then went back for his shields. Once he had everything he needed outside, he left the key in the roof access door, shut it, and got into position.

According to Penny, Death would be walking through that door, and he would have Sarah with him.

Russell waited around the corner from the roof access door in the cold wind.

He waited for Sarah to come out.

He waited to deal with Death.

But most of all, he waited to see Penny.

That made him smile for the first time in months.

Chapter 44

THE DRIVER STOPPED AT an alleyway entrance and cut the lights. "We're here," he said.

"Get out." Death pushed Sarah toward the door.

The driver jumped out and stood by the door as Sarah exited the vehicle, the pain in her ribs sharp.

Death got out behind her, the gun steady in his hand. He brought his right wrist up to examine it in the light. After moving it up and down slightly, he declared it not broken.

"Here, take this and keep it concealed." Death handed the driver the gun. "Shoot her in the face if she tries anything. And don't worry about hitting me. Just make sure you shoot her."

The driver nodded.

"Now, give me my long knife."

The driver handed Death a blade that looked like a small machete.

"Move."

The trio walked toward a side door access to the hotel.

"How are you going to get past security?" Sarah asked.

"That's all worked out."

At the door, Death ran a card by a key reader. The door clicked and opened.

It was at least one in the morning. The hallway was empty, and no sounds emitted from any of the rooms. All Sarah had to do was scream, wake people up and run. But she knew she'd get shot for her efforts.

At the end of the hallway, they waited at an elevator. The custom-made doors opened to a plush elevator car. Sarah entered the elevator. She had to do something because there was no way she was going out onto the roof just to be thrown off.

They came on behind her and hit a button.

"There's a man who haunts the eighth floor of this hotel," Death said. "Did you know that?"

Sarah shook her head.

"There have been sightings of a ghost of a grey-haired man who appears in a jacket and slacks as he moves along the hallway. Some of the staff still refuse to go to the eighth floor when working the midnight shift."

"Wow," the driver said.

"And what about the employee who hung himself off the stairwell railing on the nineteenth floor?"

"Why the history lesson?" Sarah asked.

"Just wondering if you will be haunting the building after we leave."

The elevator slowed, then stopped, and the doors opened.

"Go." Death pushed Sarah hard. The driver led them

along the hall. They entered a door to the stairs and climbed.

At any time, she could fight, but the pain in her ribs would slow her down, even if she ignored it. She'd get cut if she went after the driver with the gun. If she went for Death, she'd get shot. She had to wait for the right moment.

At the top of the stairs, they came to a door that said roof access. She examined the area.

"There's a motion sensor in that corner and a camera right there," Sarah said, pointing at it. "And you still think you're going to get away with this?"

"They're turned off." He wagged a finger in her face. "I'm not as stupid as you think. I've got people."

He turned to the access door.

"See, he even left the key in the door for me."

Death opened the door and stepped out onto the roof. The driver pushed Sarah through. The bitter wind hit her first. Then the bright red light from the hotel sign. It cast a red glow onto everything.

Death turned to the driver. "Aim that gun at Sarah."

The driver did.

"Now check that the safety is off."

The driver did.

"Good. Now, make sure when you shoot her, you don't miss, or I will gut you. Understand?"

"Absolutely."

"Good. Now, Sarah, come for a walk with me to the edge. I have something to show you."

He lowered his blade to the side and gestured with his arm. Sarah realized her last chance was to put Death between her and the driver and have the driver shoot, using Death's body as a shield. Or push him over the edge before he could push her and hope the driver ran out of bullets before one of them killed her.

Her stomach flipped. After all the training Aaron had given her in close-quarters combat, fighting with her hands and feet, how could this have gone so far?

"Aren't you coming?" Death asked.

Sarah walked with Death to the edge of the roof.

Chapter 45

RUSSELL WATCHED AS THE two men talked to Sarah. Then they walked to the edge of the roof.

What the hell are they doing?

He followed, a garbage can shield in each hand. The man with Sarah looked rugged, like a fighter. In the dark, Russell could barely make out his face.

Who would tattoo their face?

He got within four feet of the man holding the gun and slowed. At the edge of the roof, Sarah and the other man were talking. Russell lowered himself to the ground and waited a heartbeat.

How this played out would be up to Sarah. He didn't want to interrupt early, but she was in danger.

He edged closer to the man with the gun, making sure his metal garbage can lids didn't scrape or touch anything.

Then the man with Sarah did something crazy. He

grabbed her arms and tried to push her over the edge. Sarah reacted like Russell had never seen a woman move.

The man in front of him aimed at Sarah.

Russell stood up behind him and swung the garbage can lid as hard and as fast as he could.

He was too late. The gun fired before he made contact.

Chapter 46

"Lovely evening, isn't it, Sarah?" Death asked as he swept a hand over Toronto far below.

"You didn't bring me up here to be romantic. Why the small talk? Nervous?"

He closed his eyes. Tension played across his face until a tic developed beneath his right eye. "I want to know what you were doing in that massage parlor." He opened his eyes and glared at her. The tic stopped. "I want to know why you had a gun and why you shot Juan."

Sarah checked the driver to see how close he was and then crossed her arms. She had seconds to play this out.

"You're kidding, right?" she asked. "You had me chained up for almost a week. We talked daily, and not once did you ask me that. What is this? Building up the nerve to do what you came here to do? You want a solid reason? Don't worry, I'll make it easy for you to hate me." She stepped closer to him and unlocked her arms. "You're a pussy. A fucking coward who hides behind his gang. One-on-one, I'd kick your ass. Lose the weapons, and you're a nobody. Actually, that's not true. You're a low-life scum who likes to beat on women and use the gang as a reason to take sex whenever you want it. You're nothing more than a Neanderthal, and the sooner your kind are dead and gone, the sooner the rest of us will be happier." She moved her face closer to his and lowered her voice. "There, that gives you a reason to do what you came here to do?"

He looked her up and down, hatred playing across his face. "I wanted to see if we could make a truce."

"A truce? You have got to be joking."

"I could use someone like you on my side. You could be the alpha female. But now, that will never happen."

"If you don't push me off this roof, I think I'll just jump."

Death dropped his blade to the floor beside him, never taking his eyes off her. He grabbed her above the elbow with his good hand and shoved her hard toward the railing.

But Sarah was prepared. Even though she knew a bullet would welcome her efforts, she wrapped her arm around his in a way that her hand came up by his underarm. Then she yanked her arm sideways, which twisted Death's elbow up, almost snapping it.

In a rolling hip move, she drove her opposing knee up and into Death's stomach. He keeled over with a loud grunt. Still holding his arm, she twisted his body in front of her and wrapped him in an arm lock, both his arms aimed at the sky, putting him between her and the driver.

The gun fired.

She breathed again when nothing hit her. Continuing to defend herself against the shooter with Death's body, she kept him in front as she pushed toward the driver.

Death tried to spin around, but unless he dropped to the ground, he couldn't get out of Sarah's firm grip. Sure, he was a street fighter, but with his arms locked, the way she had him made it near impossible to turn around.

But then the driver's body collapsed in front of them and dropped to the floor of the roof.

Her cousin stood behind the driver.

"Russell? What are you doing here?" Sarah shouted.

Then Death dropped to his knees, twisted around, and brought a fist up and into her ribs that were already on fire.

She grunted and tried to get away from him. He hit again and then again before she could get far enough away.

The pain leveled her. She fell to her knees, knowing she had to get up and move, or she would die.

Death dove toward the railing. He came back up with his blade in his good hand.

She launched off her knees and tried to scramble away, but Death marched past her, headed for Russell.

"Look out," she tried to yell, but the pain in her ribs constricted her lungs, and it came out too low for Russell to hear.

She used the wall of the stairwell access to pull herself up and watched as Death swung his blade at Russell, an animal-like screech emitting from his mouth.

Russell pulled a round silver object up, like a shield, and met the approaching knife. Frustrated, Death tried again at a different angle, but a second shield came up just as fast.

Sarah started for the driver's body. He had the gun.

Her breath came in shallow gulps. Death was hitting and kicking Russell now. Somehow he managed to get one of the shields away from Russell.

She was almost at the driver.

The two men circled around for a moment, staring at each other. Russell had been cut. There was blood on his face.

Sarah bent to retrieve the gun.

But it was gone.

She searched frantically where the body had dropped, but it must have been kicked away.

It was nowhere in sight.

Over her shoulder, she saw Death lunge with the blade. Russell moved left to avoid it, but Death had anticipated the move. The shield was no help as the blade embedded itself in Russell's shoulder, dropping down at least four inches.

Death tugged on the handle, but all he did was jerk Russell's shoulder. The blade had stuck in bone.

Russell snapped the remaining shield down on Death's bad hand. Death screamed and held his arm up, his wrist dangling at an impossible angle.

Death wobbled on his feet and stumbled to the railing at the edge of the roof. He held on to stay on his feet.

Russell turned to her and tried to smile through immense pain.

"It's okay, Sarah," he said. "I love you. This is my parting gift. Penny said it was time I came home. Time I came to see her."

"No!" Sarah shouted.

Russell took a step toward Death at the railing, who continued to moan.

"Goodbye, Sarah."

He pulled an envelope out of his pocket and tossed it to the floor a few feet from her.

"My final request," he said and took another step.

"Russell," Sarah shouted. "Don't!"

Then he faced Death and took a step forward, the small machete still stuck in his shoulder.

A second later, he ran.

"Noooo," Sarah screamed through the pain, but he was going too fast.

Russell hit Death hard and lifted him just enough to clear the railing.

It took one second for the two men to balance over the top, then disappear. And like that, they were gone. All that remained was Death's scream.

She would remember that scream for a long time.

The scream of Death.

Chapter 47

SARAH SAT GINGERLY, EVER mindful of her sore ribs. Lyson sat across from her at his desk and adjusted things, moving his phone, setting a pen on the side.

"This is my last week here," he said. "I didn't think this day would come for a long time."

Sarah grinned. "I'm happy for you. It must've been a long distinguished career. And to go out with such a bang …"

"Funny." He stopped adjusting things. His face turned serious. "How's Aaron?"

"He's okay. Happy the charges were dropped."

"I'm happy to have retrieved my weapon without it used in a homicide. That would've marred my retirement."

"It almost was." She shrugged, not caring what he thought. Had she found the gun that night, she would have used every bullet on Death's face, and maybe Russell would still be here.

Not many people showed up at the funeral. His body was transported back to the States for burial. She hoped he found the peace he had been looking for. Maybe now he could be with his daughter and have the happiness that he couldn't have in life.

"Since you left your statement and Aaron left his, the investigation into the Leap Year Killer is over. His last two victims were released from the hospital and are having to learn sign language because of what he did to them." He picked up his pen and tapped it on his desk. "The good news is, we continued our raids on the Angels of Violence hangouts, rounding up almost one hundred members in the Toronto area alone, charging them with over three hundred charges. The Integrated Gun and Gang Task Force in Toronto feels that the Toronto chapter has been dissolved, thanks to you."

"And Russell and Aaron. I didn't do this alone."

She hardly knew Russell, but she grieved his loss. The note he left behind for her was very clear in its instructions. She only hoped he was right.

"What's next for you, Sarah?"

"The road."

"The road?"

"Can't stay too long in one place."

They were wasting time, and she knew it. The FBI had a plan and an offer for her. Russell talked about it in the note.

"There's someone who would like to see you."

"Oh yeah?" she said, acting surprised. "Who might that be? Agent Kierian?"

The creases in Lyson's forehead dipped briefly, then righted.

"Yes. How did you know?"

She smiled wide. "I'm psychic, don't you remember?"

Looking unsettled, Lyson muttered something and stood. "I'll send him in." He walked around his desk to Sarah. "You're quite the young lady, Sarah Roberts." He reached out his hand and shook hers. "Thanks for coming on board and helping as you did. And thank Aaron for me, even though he won't come down here."

"He's a little pissed, but I'm sure he'll get over it."

He released her hand and left. Her ribs ached too much to turn around. A minute later, the door opened and closed again.

Kierian stood in front of her. His face had healed nicely, leaving only a few pink spots that would turn into small scars.

"Hello, Sarah."

"Kierian."

"I wanted to talk to you—"

"I accept."

Kierian stopped and faced her. "You haven't heard what I want yet."

"Then go ahead and tell me because I'm tired and want to sleep before my flight."

"Your flight?"

"Stop fucking around, Kierian. I'm going to Rome, Italy, aren't I?"

"Well, yes, if you accept—"

"I just told you I do."

"Okay, you're going too fast for me." He sat in Lyson's chair.

"The FBI wants to propose an offer to you."

Sarah didn't respond. She didn't know all the details of the offer, but Russell had said in his note that he saw her in Rome under their protection within weeks. He said that she would die before her next birthday in April if she didn't take their offer. He couldn't see past that. At least that's what Penny told him to tell her.

"We have certain problems in Rome that we're working on with the Italian authorities. Actually, it's more their problem, but it has to do with an American, so they've called us for help. Our offer is this: if you come on board, you'll be under our protection. It'll be like you're a member of the FBI, albeit in an advisory capacity. I've been ordered to be your handler, your contact. We would work together on future cases."

"No, I work alone. Whatever Vivian tells me to do, I do it. Then I'll tell you what I did. However it shapes up, I work alone. We will not be partners."

He raised a palm in surrender. "Fine, we don't work together physically, but we *work* together. In the eyes of my bosses, you're with me in the field. You report to me. I'm your contact."

"You won't like that," she muttered.

"What?"

"Nothing."

"I can assure you, you won't be left out in the cold. If something happens, you'll have backup, you'll have resources and a weapon if needed."

"Really, a weapon too?"

"If needed."

"Tell me something," Sarah said, leaning forward a little. "Do you believe in Vivian yet, or do you still think I'm the psychic one?"

He looked out the window. After a long moment, he turned back.

"It's not important what I believe in. I've had to evaluate my beliefs and examine them recently. What I came up with is that it's plausible there's a prime mover, a Yahweh, a God."

"I'm not talking about a biblical God. I want to know if you believe in the other side. Call it Heaven if you want, but there's something, and it's good, and it helps. Do you agree? I'll know if you're lying."

He stared at her and said, "Vivian proved her existence to me when you asked for the bomb-sniffing dogs. No one knew about the bombs, not even you. I could tell that you didn't even know why you were asking for it, just that it was something written in your psychic notes. The way Russell called and warned you, and then he knew to check into that hotel two days before you showed up on the roof. And to bring the garbage can lids." He nodded a few times. "There's something out there I don't understand, but just because I don't understand it doesn't mean it doesn't exist. So, now I'm a believer."

Sarah leaned back and winced at the sharp pain that shot across her ribs. Death had snapped two of the lower ones with his knuckles. They were healing nicely but still ached when she turned a certain way.

"I believe you," she said.

He reached inside his jacket and pulled out plane tickets, slapping them on the desk in front of her.

"Your flight to Rome is two weeks away. That'll give you enough time to organize your affairs and be ready. Do you speak any Italian?"

"None."

"Learn some. You might need it."

She slipped the tickets off the desk and set them on her lap. "Payment?"

"Considerable as a consultant. Deposited into an account of your choice. Oh, and how is Aaron going to take this?"

"Smashingly."

"Keep all this confidential. The guy we're going to Italy for is connected. His name is Sam 'The Dealer' Marconi."

"What's he done that garnered the interest of the FBI?"

"He's murdered a few high-level Costra Nostra men."

"Like a mafia hitman?"

"Yes, but he's gone astray."

"Why are the Italian authorities asking for your help?"

"Because Sam Marconi is American. They've asked for us to come to pick up our boy."

"American? With a name like that?"

"Italian parents. Born here, though. Lived in Italy since he was a child. Grew up on the streets of Napoli. I'll give you the file when we're on the plane. Just keep the fact that you're going to Italy between you and Aaron."

"I don't advertise to the world what I do. I'm not on Facebook, you know. But why the secrecy in Toronto? Is he that connected?"

Kierian leaned back in Lyson's chair. "We were tasked to pick this guy up a year ago."

"So?"

"The four agents who went to Italy all came back in body bags. So far, no one has made it home alive. I volunteered, but only if I could take you. Now that you've agreed, we fly out in two weeks."

"Great."

Chapter 48

Aaron set his wine glass down on the counter so hard Sarah thought he broke it.

"Are you kidding me?"

Sarah had wondered what his response would be. She'd prepared an authentic Italian meal down to the wine, a Brunello Di Montalcino, from the Tuscan region. By prepared a meal, that meant she had heated the store-bought lasagna in the oven, an organic one, with extra meat.

"Look, I know this isn't what you wanted to hear," Sarah said. "But raising your voice will only piss me off. You don't want my last ten days in Toronto with me beating on you."

"You won't be beating anyone with those ribs. I'm not worried." He left the kitchen. "Come on. We'll talk in the living room."

She followed him. He stood by the large window that looked onto the balcony. It was snowing again.

"When were you planning on telling me?" Aaron asked.

"Uhm, now. What kind of question is that? I just told you."

He turned around to face her. She walked over and plopped down in the recliner.

"Sarah, look what happened to your cousin. To us. We were almost killed in that warehouse. If I hadn't knocked Martin onto you, that concrete piece that cut him in half would've killed you. Are you sure you still want this life?"

"Am I sure?" she gasped. "Am I sure? Haven't I been doing this for the past six-plus years? You knew that walking in."

"Okay, fair enough, but Rome?"

"I'm sure there'll be stops in Toronto along the way. Also, vacations. Besides, I'm not moving to Italy. I just have a job there."

"I can't come with you. I can't drop my classes."

"I didn't ask you to. They gave me a ticket, not you."

"I know, I know, but I wasn't sure if you made dinner and, well, you know, tried to make me think a certain way."

She squinted her eyes at him. "Come on. When am I manipulative? You forget who you're talking to."

"So, a long-distance relationship? Is that it?"

"Aaron, I have to do this. Here." She handed him Russell's note.

He opened it and read everything.

"When were you going to show me this?"

She sipped her wine. "You're not really asking inane questions again, are you? Do I have to answer that?"

"So I guess that's it?"

"Aaron, have you heard of a man named Martin Luther

King?"

"What? Of course. Why?"

"He said, 'All that needs to happen for evil to prevail is that good men do nothing.'" She paused to let it sink in. "I'm a good person. I cannot stand it when horrible people take and steal from others, hurting or killing them. With Vivian, if I can do something, then why the hell not?"

He nodded and moved to the couch.

"He also said," she continued, "the day we see the truth and cease to speak is the day we begin to die. Injustice anywhere is a threat to justice everywhere. Do you understand? That's why my mouth gets me in so much trouble."

He grabbed the colored cube on the coffee table beside him and held it up. "It takes an average of about sixty to seventy attempts to solve a Rubik's Cube. If done right, any Rubik's Cube combination can be solved in seventeen turns." He set the cube down. "That's you."

"How so?" she asked and sipped her wine.

"You're that puzzling for me, but I keep trying to figure you out, understand you. With each try, I get closer. One day, when I know you even more, it'll only take me about a dozen tries to get it. But you've helped this time. You're right. You have to go." He held Russell's note up. "Forget that Russell said you'd be dead if you didn't, I still think you should go. It's the right thing for you. It's who you and Vivian have become."

That softened her heart, tears welling in her eyes. To avoid him seeing them, she leaned forward and set her glass down.

"Be careful trying to understand women. Women

understand women and hate each other."

He laughed.

"There are statues all over the world," Sarah said. "What historical figure has more statues representing them than any other?"

"I have no idea."

"Joan of Arc. In France alone, there are roughly forty thousand of them. Now there's a young woman who fought for what she thought was right and died young doing it. Now, mind you, I'm not likening myself to her, nor do I want to die young, but that stands for something, and so do I."

He got up from the couch and sat opposite her on the edge of the coffee table. He took her hand in his.

"Sarah, I'm just overly worried I'm going to lose you, and I'm selfish. I want you all to myself. You can understand that, right?"

She nodded.

"Go, see the world. But do something for me."

"What's that?"

"Stay safe and kick some ass."

She smiled and leaned back in her chair, tears in her eyes.

"You think this is easy for me?" she asked. "I'm in love with you, Aaron. But I can't be held down right now. I've got work to do. I'm an official consultant to the FBI now. This is my time to nab as many assholes as I can, and Vivian is on board. We all must make sacrifices, and I'm prepared to make mine."

"People go off to war all the time," Aaron said. "This is just a different kind."

"Exactly. Now, take me to bed and remind me why we do this shit."

"What shit?"

"Relationships. Or should I call it relationshit?"

They stood at the same time and walked hand in hand down the hall to the bedroom.

A chapter in Sarah's life was closing, and a new one was opening. She hoped Rome would be good to her. She hoped the FBI would step up when she needed them to. Maybe they would renew a little faith in law enforcement.

As soon as they were undressed, her cell phone rang.

"Leave it," Aaron said. "I've still got you for ten days."

"Let me at least see who's calling."

Sarah picked up the phone Kierian had given her. Call display said it was him.

"Shit, I have to take this. It's Kierian."

"Great, he's already taking you from me."

"Don't be like that. It doesn't add to your masculinity."

She flicked the button and held it to her ear.

"Sarah?"

"Yeah."

"Where are you? What are you doing?"

She snuck a glance at Aaron. "Really? That's how you tell me why you've called? By asking me what I'm doing?"

"Russell Anderson. That's your cousin, right?"

Her interest piqued, she turned from Aaron and stepped to the bedroom window.

"What about it?" she whispered.

"I got a letter. I was in my office, going through my mail, and found one with no return address."

"And?"

"It said that you cannot be at Aaron's apartment on a certain date."

She turned back to Aaron, who shrugged at her. "What date? Did it mention a time?"

"Sarah, I have a car en route. They're about twenty minutes out."

"What else did it fucking say?" she shouted into the phone. "Tell me everything."

"It said if you're found in Aaron's apartment tonight, at" —he paused—"right now, that the advance team would win."

"Advance team?" she said as she stumbled across the bedroom looking for her clothes.

"The American I told you we're supposed to deal with in Rome has discovered somehow that you're working with us and that we're going to Rome. He's sent a team of men to neutralize you."

"What?" she shouted into the phone. "A team? Neutralize me? And how would he know this kind of information? Did you talk? How does he fucking know?"

"I don't know," Kierian shouted back. She detected panic in his voice. "All I know is what this letter from Russell said. Are you there right now?"

"Yes."

She found her panties and jeans and tried to get dressed with the phone jammed between her cheek and her shoulder.

"Get out. Get out now."

"I'm going. Take it easy. But I'm going to have questions for you. Someone has to pay for this. I'm seriously pissed now."

"I agree. I'm already on it."

"Is Aaron in danger?"

"Only if he's there tonight."

She ended the call and tossed the phone on the bed.

"Get dressed. We're leaving."

"I'm not going anywhere."

Sarah bolted across the room, her ribs protesting, and jammed Aaron back against the wall. "You are leaving, and you will do it my way, or you will be in danger."

"Is that what Vivian wrote?"

She stepped back, stunned. "What?"

"When I came home earlier today, and you were sleeping, there was a piece of paper and a pen on the bed beside you. I put it over there."

The paper sat beside the pen on the top of Aaron's dresser. Sarah lunged over the bed and grabbed it.

Do not stay at Aaron's tonight. Find a hotel. Then move underground until your flight to Rome. The team sent to remove you will be in Rome days later. You'll deal with them on Italian soil.

"And you never thought to tell me about this?" she asked as she tossed it to him.

As he read it, she grabbed her shirt and slipped into it.

"I didn't read it," Aaron said. "I thought I'd show it to you tonight after dinner." He looked up, still naked. "How did Kierian know?"

"Russell's daughter knew this would happen." She flicked her hand at the note. "So she had Russell send a letter to Kierian. Lucky for us, he got to his mail in time. He's sending a car. They'll be here in—"

There was a loud knock on the door.

"Shit, hurry up," Sarah whispered. "Get dressed."

Aaron grabbed his jeans and hopped into them.

The knock came again.

Aaron grabbed his sweater as Sarah moved to the

bedroom door and waited.

"Nobody threatens me in my own apartment. I'm going to open that door and teach them a—"

Sarah spun on him and pushed him against the wall again. "You want to die? You have a death wish? If we could win here tonight, Vivian would've said something. When she says vacate the premises, that's what it means. Now, follow me. We're leaving."

Aaron followed her down the hall and into the living room.

They knocked harder. Something big banged against the door.

Sarah slid the balcony door open and stepped out. It was a few weeks until spring, but the balcony was cleared of snow. The jump would only be about ten feet.

Both of them climbed onto the railing and stopped to look at each other.

Something banged inside the apartment.

Sarah looked back and saw the entire lock mechanism and door handle blast off the door. Then it was smashed open.

At least seven masked men ran inside, each turning down the hall and into the kitchen, large guns in their hands.

She looked at Aaron, smiled, and shrugged.

"Such is my life."

Then she teetered over and was lost in the air.

About Jonas Saul

Jonas Saul is the bestselling author of the Sarah Roberts Series—more than two million sold!—and has written and published over sixty thrillers. After acquiring an agent, he signed several deals in Los Angeles, with MadRiver Pictures optioning his Sarah Roberts Series— over forty books!—(currently in development).

Jonas has often outranked Stephen King and Dean

Koontz on Amazon over the past decade. He's regularly invited to be a guest speaker, teacher, or workshop presenter at international writing conferences and film festivals worldwide. He hosts an annual writer's retreat in Greece, where he currently lives. He focuses his teaching on how to get tension and emotion in every scene, on every page, how he made it as a creator/writer, the path to success in this business, and the pitfalls to avoid. He also hosts a reading retreat in Greece with guest authors, yoga retreats, and hiking retreats. Visit the Imagine Greece Retreats website at www.imaginegreeceretreats.com, or email him directly to discuss an opportunity to join one of the retreats at jonas@imaginegreeceretreats.com.

Jonas is also a professional freelance editor. He works for several publishers and does private editing for clients, with many testimonials on his website at www.imaginepress.org, which details each author's response to Jonas's editing skills. Email Jonas directly for an editing quote at editor@imaginepress.org.

To book Jonas for a speaking engagement at a writer's conference/festival, to have him on your jury at a film festival, or even to say hello, email Jonas directly at jonassaul@icloud.com.

For updates on releases, hit the "Follow" button on Amazon or Bookbub, and join Jonas on Facebook, where he's most active.

Contact Jonas Saul

Linktree: Find me here

Email: jonassaul@icloud.com

www.ingramcontent.com/pod-product-compliance
Lightning Source LLC
Chambersburg PA
CBHW022104310726
48972CB00007B/1869